Treasure Trove Antiques

THE LUCKY CAT

L.M. SOMERTON

The Lucky Cat
ISBN # 978-1-83943-912-4
©Copyright L.M. Somerton 2020
Cover Art by Louisa Maggio ©Copyright September 2020
Interior text design by Claire Siemaszkiewicz
Pride Publishing

THE LUCKY CAT

Dedication

With thanks and love to Paul and Will.

Chapter One

Sometimes there were advantages to being vertically challenged. Landry, his ass sticking out from under a seventeenth-century folding card table, paused to contemplate other occasions when his five-feet-six-inch stature had been of benefit. Not when attempting to get served at his favorite leather bar, though getting squished between all those black-clad hunks was always bearable. He snorted. Not when reaching for his preferred brand of chips at the market, which were always on the top shelf. Put there, he was sure, by the snotty assistant manager as revenge for Landry turning down his offer of a quick blow job in the staff restroom. *As if.* Never at family meals when he got to sit between his older twin brothers like a blond munchkin between two extras from *Vikings*. He reversed, wiggling his back end to avoid a willow-patterned platter balancing on a brass coal scuttle. His knees ached and he'd banged his elbow on a cast-iron fireguard, but he had rescued the battered cannonball making an escape attempt beneath teetering piles of stock.

"Well, there's a pretty sight."

"Hey!" Landry went for indignant rather than flattered. He tried to get up too soon and banged his head on solid, woodworm-free oak. "Fuck me!" He finally made it to open air and scrambled to his feet, rubbing his already messy hair into further disarray.

"Is that a request?"

Landry looked up…and up…into a pair of twinkling pale-blue eyes. The customer, because that was who Landry guessed the newcomer must be, was drop-dead, my-ass-is-yours gorgeous and he was grinning. Well, smirking.

"Funny man. What can I help you with, *sir*?" Landry gritted his teeth and remembered that Mr. Lao, his boss, would swat him like a bug if he snarked at a potential patron. *Though, on this occasion, it might be worth it to mess with the man.*

"Another leading question."

Landry rolled his eyes. Black hair, blue eyes and a stubbled, chiseled chin did not equate to a free pass. "The massage parlor is three doors down, just before St. Peter's. You can get a full-body whatever then confess all in the space of an hour." He made an ineffective attempt to brush dust from the knees of his ripped black jeans. Blue Eyes reached into his jacket and produced a wallet, which he opened to display a Seattle PD badge and ID card.

"Gage Roskam. Is your boss around?"

Landry was more turned on than intimidated by the badge. Cop plus handcuffs equaled sexy time. Every cop he'd ever met had had a 'don't fuck with me' attitude and a natural bent for control—just the type of man Landry liked to mess with. He batted his lashes. "And what makes you think I'm not the boss?"

"You're not a sixty-eight-year-old Chinese guy by the name of Jian Lao?"

"Very observant, Officer. All that training paid off." Landry put an extra bit of swing into his hips as he walked toward the cash desk at the rear of the shop.

"Putting your tax dollars to work, brat."

"Hey! Aren't you supposed to call me sir, what with you being a public servant and all?"

"In your dreams, and you should show more respect for law enforcement."

"Gonna make me?"

"You're lucky I'm on duty or I'd bend you over the nearest flat surface and give you the spanking you're begging for."

"Is that line in the big bad cop manual?" Landry scuttled behind the cash desk, relieved that it reached to his waist and therefore hid his burgeoning erection. "Because I don't think it's very professional."

"I use language appropriate to the situation." Gage grinned. "I can give you my badge number if you wanna make a complaint. Then again, if you'd like to engage in a deep and meaningful conversation about your attitude, you can use this number." He grabbed a pen from a pot next to the cash register then scribbled his number on the top sheet of the pile of wrapping tissue.

Landry nibbled on his lower lip. He got propositioned a lot but there was something about Gage that appealed to him. He might as well have had 'Dominant' tattooed across his forehead, and that pushed all Landry's submissive buttons. He'd also called Landry out on his snarky attitude, which had the dual effect of stimulating Landry's intellect as he decided on the most appropriate retort *and* giving him the urge to drop to his knees. He resisted the latter option.

"Now you're the one who's dreaming. Mr. Lao isn't here." Landry checked his watch. "And as he headed out to lunch with a bunch of cronies from his bowling club, I don't expect him back any time soon. So is there anything I can help you with that won't involve me getting arrested?"

Gage gave him an intense look, which made Landry squirm and wish he'd put on a looser pair of pants that morning. "Fine. I have some pictures I want you to take a look at." Gage pulled out his phone.

"How kinky are they?" Landry asked. "Because I think you should know there's some stuff I'm just not into."

"Only *some* stuff? You do surprise me. Are you into receiving stolen goods?"

"No! Of course not." Landry bristled. "Treasure Trove Antiques is a reputable establishment. Mr. Lao doesn't buy anything without checking out its provenance and I don't buy anything at all because Mr. Lao won't let me yet. I can't tell the difference between Ming dynasty and tourist trash made in some underground sweatshop in Kowloon, though he is trying to teach me. I'm kind of his apprentice."

"If I show you a bunch of pictures, would you know whether you have the items in stock?"

"That I can do." Landry couldn't help but preen a little. "Mr. Lao has trouble remembering what day of the week it is. He relies on me to be able to lay my hands on anything the customers are looking for, and in this place…" He gestured at the cavernous space piled high with row upon row of stock. "That's nothing short of miraculous."

"Then is there somewhere we can sit, because this may take a while?"

"I'll have an extra-large, skinny, vanilla latte and a brownie."

Gage sighed. "You're lucky I'm a patient man. Where do you suggest I go for those?"

"Now that depends." Landry tapped a finger against his lips. "You don't look like a Starbucks man, but there's one down the block if that floats your boat. The café next door is a small independent place and there's not much I wouldn't do for a regular supply of their baked goods."

"What does a Starbucks man look like? No, don't tell me. I don't need to know."

"My cooperation is contingent on provisions."

"So you're telling me you accept bribes?"

"Absolutely. So long as they involve chocolate. Or coffee. Preferably both and in large quantities."

"I'll be five minutes. Don't go anywhere."

"Perhaps you should cuff me, Officer." Landry blinked.

"It's Detective, and don't tempt me." Gage strolled toward the exit. Landry kept his gaze glued to the man's ass, wishing that his jacket didn't cover it quite so well. He licked his lips and pushed the heel of his hand against his erection.

"Down boy. Behave. You're going to get me into so much trouble... Not that I wouldn't enjoy engaging in a little crime and punishment role play with Detective Roskam."

A carved, Middle Eastern table not far from the cash desk would allow Landry to keep an eye on the register while he helped out Mr. Hot Detective. He dragged a couple of sturdy 1930s chairs down an aisle, setting them behind the table. He also directed the battered Anglepoise lamp on one corner of the cash desk toward the table to give a bit more light, because Mr. Lao kept the place in semi-darkness in the hope that some of the customers wouldn't look too closely at what they were buying.

There were a few people browsing the aisles and Landry rang up a purchase for a young couple who'd found a pressed-glass art deco vase for a parent's birthday. He'd just finished wrapping it, having been careful to preserve the sheet of tissue with Gage's number on it, when Gage returned carrying a cardboard tray of coffee and a paper bag. Landry eyed them, happy to see they came from the café next door. He wished his departing customers well then made a grab for the bag, poking his nose inside to find two sizeable brownies, double chocolate chip cookies and two white chocolate and blueberry muffins.

"Color me impressed," Landry muttered around a mouthful of brownie. "Oh my God, this is so good."

"Anyone would think you hadn't been fed for a week." Gage set the coffees on the table. He slipped off his jacket and hung it on the back of one of the chairs.

Landry couldn't help but admire the way his shirt pulled tight across his broad chest. *The man is fit! I would pay good dollars to take a peek beneath that cotton.* "Hey, don't judge. I woke up late because I forgot to set my alarm and didn't have time for breakfast. Normally I'd sneak next door, but Mr. Lao went out before I got the chance and I can't leave this place unattended. He has spies everywhere and he'd know, even if I only locked up for five minutes. There's a kettle in the back but he only keeps tea. Tea! The man is deranged. He thinks coffee belongs in satanic rituals. There's something seriously wrong with him. He bought the kettle in England when he was there on a buying trip and now he gets tea sent over every few months because he fell in love with some brand he can't buy here."

"Have you finished?" Gage sat down, adjusting the chair so he could stretch out his legs, crossing them at the ankles.

"Why, do you have somewhere more interesting to be?" Landry pouted.

"I'm pretty sure I could find somewhere less frustrating to spend time." Gage handed over one of the coffees. "Here's your concoction."

"I suppose you think it's unmanly to drink anything but strong black stuff." Landry removed the lid of his cup and breathed in the sweet aroma. "You should try this. It might improve your temper."

Gage took one of the cookies from the bag. "I'm plenty sweet enough for you."

"Is that so? And what makes you think I'm interested in sweet men?"

"I'd guess that's the last thing you're interested in, or need. A brat like you requires a firm hand."

From Gage's tone, Landry guessed he'd be more than happy to provide that hand. "And there you go again with the inappropriate comments. Don't you have some pictures to show me?"

"We can pick up the discussion about your need for discipline later, when I'm off duty." Gage put his phone on the table. "Swipe left. Stop if you see something you recognize. It's a work phone, not personal, so don't get excited."

An array of antiques danced in front of Landry's eyes as he scrolled through Gage's extensive gallery of pictures. Oil paintings followed porcelain followed furniture and jewelry. "I don't recognize anything…" Landry kept scrolling but much of the inventory was far too high-end for Mr. Lao. "Some of this stuff is absolutely gorgeous. The boss comes up with some great pieces, but this is way beyond his budget. Wait…" Landry went back to the picture of a gold and amethyst necklace. Dating from the early 1900s, it looked familiar. "This one… The lighting isn't great but I think we might have this. Oh God, is the boss in trouble?" His heart fell. Mr. Lao had been good to him.

"Can you lay your hands on it?" Gage asked.

"Sure. Just give me a minute." Landry shoved his chair back. Most of the decent jewelry was kept in a locked cabinet in the far corner of the store, behind two bookcases full of first editions. Mr. Lao always stashed stock that might tempt a smash and grab in the least accessible parts of the shop. Shimmying his way between teetering piles of furniture, Landry took the cabinet's key from his pocket. The necklace was on the bottom shelf, nestling on the black velvet lining of its leather-covered box. Seeing it again, Landry knew it was identical to the one in the picture. He took it from its place, relocked the cabinet then dragged his feet a bit getting back to Gage. "Here it is."

"That's the one." Gage pushed the box back to Landry before taking a huge bite of muffin. "These aren't bad."

"Not bad? What are you talking about? I just outed my boss as a jewel thief and all you're interested in is a muffin." Landry grabbed his coffee and took a long swig, wishing it contained a splash of rum.

"A small test of your honesty."

"You're making no sense whatsoever." Landry felt like stamping his foot but made do with scowling.

"I seeded the photographs with legal items from the various shops I've been visiting. If you hadn't picked it out, I would have suspected your motives. A colleague of mine took a picture of the necklace a few days ago."

Landry gaped. "You... You... Pain in the ass! You could have given me a heart attack."

Gage chuckled. "It was worth it to see your face. Did you know your earlobes go pink when you're nervous?"

"They do not!" Landry pulled on one soft lobe. "And quit looking at my ears, you freak." He sat down, groping in the paper bag for a cookie. "After that, you owe me coffee and baked goods every day this week."

"Wanna see me again, huh?"

"You can just drop them off." Unaccustomed to the shy, awkward feeling he was experiencing, Landry picked at the chocolate chips in his cookie.

"I don't think so. We need to go out on a date so I can explain to you how relationships between Dominants and submissives work."

"I haven't seen you around the local scene... How did you find out?"

"Research. You'd be surprised how much I know about you."

"Have you been following me?"

"On and off over the last few weeks. The department has been keeping tabs on antique store staff across the city. I took a special interest in you after hearing about some of the places you frequent. Fond of leather and latex, aren't you?" Gage lifted his coffee in a toast.

"I… Maybe?" Landry scuffed the toe of his sneaker against the parquet flooring. "Are you really a Dom, or just playing?"

"Through and through the genuine article."

Landry pictured Gage in full leather regalia. His mouth dried and his cock jerked. He didn't know where to put himself.

"What time do you close on Saturday?"

"You're the detective. You work it out."

"I hope you enjoy standing, because by the time I'm done with your rebellious ass, you won't want to sit on it. I'll pick you up here at closing time." Gage pushed his chair back, not waiting for a response. He strolled through the store like he owned the place.

Shell-shocked, Landry watched him go, wondering what had just happened. He shook his head. "No way he's gonna show." He grabbed the bag of leftover treats to take back to the counter along with his half-finished coffee. "More's the pity."

Chapter Two

Gage still had a smile on his face when he got back to his car. Landry Carran promised to be a challenge of the kind that Gage relished. He couldn't wait to tie him down then tease him until he screamed for mercy. "Happy days." He had time to make a few date arrangements before he had to meet up with his long-suffering partner and he knew the perfect place to take his brat.

My brat. Has a nice ring to it. He put the car in drive then pulled into the steady stream of traffic. His destination was only a few blocks away but he didn't want to waste time by walking there and back. The Bowline took bookings in person, no exceptions, even for him. His luck was in, because he snagged a rarer-than-hens'-teeth parking spot as someone pulled out right in front of him. The restaurant was down a narrow alley off the main drag. As always, the walkway was immaculate and smelled vaguely of Simple Green. No doubt some unfortunate sub had been out scrubbing down the concrete in case a speck of dirt had dared land there. Grinning at the thought, Gage pushed the bell next to a steel-banded door, which swung open seconds later.

"We're closed."

"I'm a detective. I worked that one out for myself." Gage smirked.

"Gage! It's been months since you graced us with your presence. Get your cute ass in here. Diego has coffee on."

"Hey, Mitch, I can't stay long. I'm working. Just stopped by to make a reservation."

"Diego will make my life a fucking misery if you don't come in, man. One coffee won't kill you, though I guess Sancha might. That squirt-sized hellion still your partner?"

"Yep, and I'm still breathing with all my bits intact. She loves me."

"She tolerates you 'cause you're pretty and you write up good reports. She told me so."

"You wanna be sleeping on the couch? Because I can turn around and leave you to explain my departure to Diego."

"I take it all back. You're ugly as sin and can barely string two words together. Better?"

"Honey, what are you doing out here?" A face peered around Mitch's bulk. "Gage, sweetie! Is this gorilla of mine keeping you on the doorstep?" Diego gave Mitch a glare. "Come in!"

"Hey, Diego." After a quick look to Mitch for permission, Gage gave Diego a hug. "Still keeping your Dom in line, I see."

"Always." Diego grabbed his hand then towed him across the hall to a glass door that granted access to the restaurant. "Take the weight off. I'll get coffee."

"Always best to just do as he says." Mitch shrugged.

There were several couches arranged around low tables where customers could wait and peruse the menus until their tables were ready. Gage parked his butt on one of them and Mitch joined him.

"So, you want to book a table?"

"Yeah, for two on Saturday night if you have one. I know I'm pushing my luck at such short notice, so don't worry if you don't have anything open."

"As it happens, we had a cancellation, so you're in luck. You know Ben Frost, right?"

Gage nodded.

"Well, as of this morning, his sub Carl has had gall bladder surgery."

"Ah, well that would put a damper on weekend plans. Still, Ben will love playing nurse for a few weeks. He's into medical kink in a big way, if I remember rightly."

"I mentioned stirrups to Diego once and, after he'd made some joke about riding a cowboy to save a horse, he regaled me with a graphic story about his sister giving birth, which he witnessed thanks to her other half being away on an oil rig at the time." Mitch shuddered. "Never going there."

Gage was saved from thinking about that any further by Diego arriving with a tray of coffee, which he placed on the table before kneeling at Mitch's side. Mitch ruffled his hair. "Thanks, love. Guess what? Gage booked a table."

"Oh! Oh wow. Who's the lucky boy?" Diego handed out their beverages.

"That would ruin the surprise, wouldn't it?" Gage sipped his drink and gave a contented sigh.

"You're mean!" Diego pouted. He had the lips for it, lush and pink. He batted his lashes over warm brown eyes.

"That might work on Mitch, but not on me." Gage smiled. "Nice try, though."

"It doesn't work on me either," Mitch whined.

"Yes, it does." Diego and Gage spoke in unison, following up with a high five.

"You know you're going to pay for that, right?" Mitch gave Diego's hair a tug, tilting his head back to give him access for a kiss. If Diego had a smart retort prepared, it was effectively silenced.

Gage watched them, a little jealous. He wanted what they had. *Well fuck.* That was a new thought. He'd never considered anything long-term before, had always been quite content to play the scene. Something had changed. *Landry.* "That little shit is in my head." He groaned. He'd only just talked to the man, and he already wanted to know so much more about him. The things he'd read about Landry, his habits, and more, had only served to heighten the desire to meet the brat. And doing that, Gage discovered that what he'd read on paper didn't even scratch the surface. Landry was funny, and it was obvious that even though he was submissive, he wasn't going to be a pushover. Not that Gage wanted that. He liked the sassy streak Landry displayed. "I said that out loud, didn't I?"

His friends stopped necking long enough to nod and give him sympathetic glances.

"You're on the precipice, my friend." Mitch patted Gage's shoulder. "It happened to me too. One day you're free and easy, letting your kink roam wild, the next some brat with mind control powers is taming you. Turning you into a domesticated Dom."

"*Dom*esticated!" Diego about fell over laughing.

Gage groaned. "I need air. I'll see you guys Saturday night." He shook Mitch's hand. "If there's any justice in this world, I'll expect Diego to be carrying a pillow with him."

"That's a sure bet." Mitch pulled Diego over his lap, working his pants down to expose his pert behind. "You can watch if you like."

"Tempting, but I gotta run or Sancha will be delivering a verbal spanking at the very least. I'll let myself out."

As he made his way toward the exit, Gage glanced around the restaurant to see if anything had changed since his last visit. As far as he knew it was the only eatery in the state, outside of the club scene, that catered specifically to the BDSM community. Every table had its quirks and they were all set in individual booths. Some were on platforms that had to be reached by steps. There were also two on a mezzanine and one in a pit. Three could be laid for a small group but most were tables for two. Plants and trellising helped provide privacy, screening the settings from each other.

Diego and Mitch only opened three nights a week. The Bowline was their hobby, their passion. Diego loved to cook but also ran his own surveying business. Mitch could burn water but traveled the world buying wine for the best hotels and restaurants in the country. They'd made their dream a reality and created a place where friends and the community could be themselves over a top-quality meal. Gage wasn't aware of anywhere else he could take a date, chain him to his seat and torture his cock while a waiter asked him to taste the wine with a completely straight face. He grinned. He couldn't wait to introduce Landry to the delights of Diego's cooking and everything else that The Bowline had to offer.

As he closed the door behind him, Gage checked his watch. "Fuck." He sprinted down the alley, dove into his car and peeled away like he'd been called to a multiple homicide. If he was late to meet his partner, his own death was assured. Sancha Hernandez was the scariest female on the planet. He loved her to bits, and she'd saved his sorry hide on more occasions than he could count, but he did not want to spend the rest of the day in a car with her in a bad mood. The last time he'd pissed her off, she'd denied him coffee for an entire night's stake out. The woman was cruel. She'd make a good Domme, but as far as Gage knew her love life was as vanilla as her favorite ice cream flavor. Her husband was a paramedic and the two of them juggled shift working and two rambunctious kids with the help of an extended family that owned a huge holiday complex in Cancun. Gage had been the beneficiary of several complimentary vacations thanks to how much Sancha's mom loved him. He was definitely her favorite, over and above her eldest daughter, probably because she had five girls and no sons. Gage was the stand-in, something he had no problem with.

He arrived at the Copper Kettle diner with three minutes to spare. As always, he parked the car in one of the staff spaces around back then made his way in through the employee entrance. Pops, the owner, traded parking for loud announcements that there were cops amongst his clientele. Mitch put the lack of crime in the area down to Pops' two hundred and fifty pound, tattooed, heavily muscled bulk and his membership of The Raiders, a local biker gang, more than his or Sancha's presence. Pops, however, was convinced that having two detectives as his best customers was good karma. His gang might have a bad-ass rep, but they were more into good deeds for the local children's hospital than tearing up the neighborhood. Pops himself cried buckets over reruns of *Lassie* and had his own pack of adopted strays that ranged from a miniature terrier cross to something that resembled a wolf.

Sancha sat in the same booth as always, facing the door. Her usual chocolate milkshake sat in front of her, untouched. That meant she hadn't long arrived because she had a tendency to inhale anything that had been in close proximity to a cocoa bean. Gage slid into the opposite seat and gave her his most disarming grin. "Hey, partner, how was your morning?"

"You're cutting it fine and my morning was…frustrating. I had no idea how much ancient furniture there was for sale in this city, or how many antique geeks. I have learned things today that I will never need to know. Were you aware, for example, that you should only clean bronze sculptures with a soft cloth, toothbrush or the nozzle brush of your vacuum cleaner? Usual waxes and polishes contain cleaning agents which can affect the patina of the bronze. I have to buy myself some Mohawk Blue Label Paste Wax, apply a thin coat then sit and look at it for six to twelve hours before polishing." She grimaced.

"Fascinating." Gage tried not to laugh. "Have you ordered yet?"

"How about some sympathy? I suppose you spent the morning fluttering your lashes at vacuous blondes and being served milk and fucking cookies."

"Not quite," Gage admitted, thinking of the blond he had met and grabbing the laminated menu. "I got through my three locations but came up with zip."

"Anyone try to hide anything from the pictures?"

"Nope. Seems like the antique dealers of this fair city are honest. At least the ones we've visited so far—or they're a lot savvier than we give them credit for. To be fair, I think I got genuine reactions this morning."

"Me too. The snooty bronze guy accused me of trying to frame him but mellowed after a bit of gratuitous flattery."

"That must have hurt." Gage chuckled.

"Oh, it did." Sancha rolled her eyes then took a long slurp of milkshake through her green and white striped straw. "I don't get paid enough for that kind of suffering."

"I appreciate your sacrifice. Where the hell's Pops?"

As if by magic, Pops ambled over to the table. He shoved a mug of coffee in Gage's direction. "Why do you bother looking at that menu, Gage?" Pops asked. "You always order the same damn thing."

"Maybe I want to mix it up a little today."

"Do you?" Pops tapped a well-chewed pen against his notepad.

"I'll take the usual." Gage sighed and put the menu down.

Sancha snorted down her straw, creating bubbles in her shake. "Green salad for me please, Pops. Extra-large curly fries and a cheeseburger on the side."

"Yes, ma'am, coming right up."

Sancha blew him a kiss and he walked away with a goofy grin on his face.

"Slut." Gage took a swig of coffee. "I've had way too much caffeine so far today."

"Is there such a thing? And yep, there's not much I won't do for one of Pops' burgers, so sue me."

Gage shook his head and pushed his mug away. "So what's the plan for this afternoon? Keep going with the antiques stores? I still have a few on my list."

"I think we have to. We need to treat them all the same and you never know what might turn up. *But,* I get the feeling these guys are several steps ahead of us. Doesn't mean we can skip the legwork. We'll reconvene back at the station this evening and decide on next steps."

"You know, I just don't get it. Why buy something so hot that you can never show it to anyone? What's the point of a painting that sits in a vault, or a piece of jewelry that no one ever wears?"

"Private collectors like these are obsessive. They'll do anything to own what they want. Just *having* it is enough. There is some serious psychological damage going on with these people. They want what no one else can have."

"Two security guards were gunned down during that exhibition heist in Tokyo. The buyers are just as guilty as the thieves."

"And the buyers are here in the good old US of A, which makes them our problem. Dealers are importing all the time. Sooner or later, we'll come across one that is less than lilywhite. What we're doing at the moment is just the sounding out process. I trust my gut. There's a lead around the corner, I know it. Now, no more shoptalk. Let's eat."

"Yes, ma'am." Gage mimicked Pops' deferential tone, knowing he was safe from Sancha's ire as their food arrived. She'd no doubt get her revenge later. In the meantime, a plate of fried chicken had his name written all over it.

* * * *

"Landry, where are you hiding?" Mr. Lao shouted.

"Peace is shattered," Landry muttered, emerging from behind a skyscraper of furniture, which had a massive oak banqueting table at the base, topped with a walnut sideboard, which in turn supported a British arts and crafts blanket box and a mahogany dressing table mirror. "I'm here, Mr. L. I was dusting." He brandished his telescopic feather duster topped with a crown of rainbow fluff, a Christmas gift from Mr. Lao the previous year. Dust motes caught in a shaft of sunlight swirled in the draft he created, swinging his duster like a cheerleader's baton.

"Good boy. Dust is the monster in the fight between good and evil. Did you sell anything while I was gone?" He polished his spectacles then peered around the store.

"Sure, it's been a good day. I cleared two pictures, a silver photograph frame, that pair of steamer chairs…"

"The ones with the woodworm?"

"Yep. The customer decided the holes added to the character of the pieces and I reassured her that any actual worms had evacuated those chairs somewhere around 1952. I also moved on that tandem bicycle to a couple planning to take it to California for a vacation, some costume jewelry and that hideous green jardinière that could have been a prop in *The Addams Family*."

"Naughty boy! You should be more respectful of the antiques, though you're right about that jardinière. It was a monstrosity and I'd given up hope of ever selling it. Who bought it?"

"A high school drama teacher wanted it as a prop in a production of *The Importance of Being Earnest*. I gave him a hefty discount."

"You mean you gave it away?"

"I…uh…maybe?"

Mr. Lao grinned. "I count it a win. I was getting to the point when I would have paid someone to take it."

"I knew you'd want to donate it. He offered to bring it back once they were finished with the production, but I told him to raffle it or something. It only got quiet in the last half-hour. Oh, and in bigger news, we also got a visit from the cops this morning, not long after you left. Some detective looking for stolen goods."

"I hope you told him that this is an honest establishment. It's taken me fifty years to build a good reputation…"

Landry tuned out the next few minutes as Mr. Lao went through his familiar diatribe about how he'd started the business from scratch with a few bits of bric-a-brac and twenty dollars. "How about you, did you have a good time with your club cronies?"

"Sure. Good food, good company… But we're all getting older, Landry. One day you'll find out what it's like to creak every time you move. All everyone talks about is their latest ailment and half of them repeat the same thing over again because they've already forgotten what they said the first time. At least I'm not losing my marbles just yet." He wandered across to the cash register, pressing the button to release the drawer. He pulled out a fifty then brought it over to Landry. "You worked hard today, covering for me. Buy yourself some of those fancy coffees you slobber over."

It was the closest thing to praise Mr. Lao ever gave. "Wow, thanks Mr. L. That's fantastic... Wait, what's the catch?" Landry flapped the bill in Mr. Lao's direction.

"Why do you have to be so suspicious all the time? You should accept gifts with grace." Mr. Lao scowled.

"Experience. You're up to something, boss. I get fair pay. Bonuses are suspect. The last time you gave me extra, you sent me to deliver that cast-iron cauldron and I almost dislocated a shoulder lugging it across town."

"Fine, you pick up some tips from that detective this morning?"

Landry's face heated and he examined the threadbare tapestry hanging on the nearest wall.

"Oh, I see... Mr. Detective was hot stuff," Mr. Lao crowed. "You wanna get in his pants?"

"I am not discussing this with you. It's more embarrassing than when my dad attempted to give me a safe gay sex talk, and quit changing the subject. What are you up to?"

"I have an invitation for an all-expenses-paid trip to Hong Kong. Eddie Chang is heading back there to sort out funeral arrangements for his father and he's asked me to go with him to help out. Chang Senior was a hundred and one and loaded. I'll have time for a few buying expeditions while I'm there."

"Sounds exciting." Landry was a little envious. "Who are you going to bring in to manage this place while you're gone?" Landry didn't mind working with other people. Mr. Lao had drafted in various family members to help over the three years Landry had worked for him.

"Actually, I was thinking you might like to do it."

"Me?" Landry gaped.

"Am I talking to any other employees at this moment?"

"You don't have any other employees."

"Not the point. Do you think you could manage on your own for three weeks? You have more than enough experience now. You could close for an hour at lunchtime, maybe a bit earlier than usual in the evenings."

"But... I don't know what to say." That Mr. Lao would trust him with his precious store meant a lot to Landry.

"'Yes' would be good. I want my trip."

"Yes!"

"No buying anything."

"No, sir."

"No stashing coffee in the kitchen."

"Pinky swear."

"No necking with hot cops behind the bookshelves."

"Well..." Landry giggled as Mr. Lao gave him a swift clip around the ear. "I won't let you down, Mr. L., I promise."

"I know you won't, Landry. You're a good boy. Sometimes. You can finish for the day now. I'll help these customers then close up. Go spend your coffee money." An elderly couple headed in their direction.

"Wait, when are you leaving?"

"Sunday."

"This Sunday? As in the day after tomorrow? I think I need a brown paper bag." Landry felt a sudden need for hard liquor.

"No hyperventilating in the store."

"Is that rule three hundred fifty-four?" Landry ducked as Mr. Lao made another swipe for him.

"Excuse me." Mr. Lao addressed the customers walking toward him, who looked a little startled. "It's hard to find good staff these days."

"Hey!" Affronted, Landry scowled. "See you tomorrow, Mr. L." He grinned to show the customers that all was well then made his way to the back of the shop where a doorway granted access to a narrow hall. There were two storerooms, a tiny kitchen and bathroom back there, as well as a set of stairs leading to the first and second floors. Mr. Lao had an apartment on the first floor and Landry a much smaller one on the second. He loved that to get to work he just had to roll out of bed, shower then trot down the stairs. A one-minute commute suited him.

At the end of a long day, the stairs were a drag. He hauled his tired ass up them, counting the steps with the creaky boards. The landing outside Mr. Lao's door smelled of incense and made Landry's sneeze. "Damn it! Every time."

It was a relief to get into his own small but cozy home, furnished with unwanted stock from the store. As a result, each room was a mishmash of styles. Landry had added a few touches of his own. He was addicted to the Indian cushion covers that his friend Prisha Midal, from the grandly titled Eastern Emporium across the street, imported. They were decorated with tiny mirrors and gold embroidery, and came in every color of the rainbow. Prisha gave him a healthy discount and had even donated a few faulty ones for free. In return, Landry referred customers to her as often as he could. The Emporium didn't stock antiques but did have a great range of hand-carved furniture and some amazing rugs that complemented the pieces that Landry sold. Most of the businesses on the street recommended each other — they all benefited and it added to the nice community feel of the area.

Landry didn't bother to lock his door. He never did. The shop had decent security and he couldn't imagine why anyone would bother to rob his place when there was a shop full of goods below him. He took a quick shower then changed into comfy sweats and a Harvard T-shirt that had been a gift from one of his brothers. His tiny galley kitchen didn't have space for a fancy coffee maker so he made up a French press, getting his usual buzz of pleasure when he pushed the plunger down to squish the grounds. He had a brownie left from earlier in the day so he settled on the couch with his laptop, a mug of coffee and his treat and proceeded to research antique crime. *Just in case Mr. Hottie shows up tomorrow night.* "Who am I kidding? He wanted something from me and knew the best way of getting it. There's no way a guy that perfect is going to be into me." Landry sighed. He ought to give Gage the benefit of the doubt. He had seemed interested and Landry didn't think anyone could fake that kind of dominance. He'd wager good money that the man was kinky through and through. He wriggled at the thought of Gage delivering a spanking with those big hands. He wondered what Gage might be into, whether they might be compatible.

Switching his mind away from bondage and CBT, Landry immersed himself in a website giving details of the biggest heists in the art world, wondering at the value of some of the paintings. When he got bored with his research, Netflix provided entertainment in the form of the Hitchcock film *To Catch a Thief*, a film about a cat burglar starring Cary Grant and Grace Kelly. By the time Landry crawled into bed that night, he was picturing a masked Gage, dressed in black, robbing the rich then returning home to express his euphoria by pounding Landry's ass. He eyed the shelf next to his bed, which housed his collection of broken and battered lucky cats. *Perhaps they'll bring me some man luck, not that they've been very successful so far.* He snuggled beneath the covers and closed his eyes. *No counting sheep for me tonight. Bring on the dreams.*

Chapter Three

For Landry, Saturday was always the least enjoyable day at Treasure Trove because it was stupid busy. Mr. Lao was a traditionalist and didn't open on a Sunday, so anyone who couldn't make it to the shop during the week made it their business to get there on a Saturday. Regular clients were supplemented with tourists, curious passers-by and general time wasters hunting a bargain they were never going to find. Mr. Lao knew his stuff. He was never going to miss a hallmark concealed by layers of dirt or mistake a genuine artwork for a fake. He had a feel for old things that Landry hoped to learn over time. For now, it was his job to fetch and carry, make nice with the customers and keep things clean and, if not tidy, only moderately hazardous. Saturday was bruise day, when every sharp-cornered lump of wood connected with his shins, hips and arms. By closing, Landry was tired, aching and grumpy. Mr. Lao had left him to lock up alone, saying it would be good practice for the next three weeks, so at precisely one minute past eight,

Landry ventured onto a fogbound street to lower the security shutters.

He shivered as the damp air soaked into his thin T-shirt. The atmosphere was eerie with visibility so poor. The streetlamps and brake lights on passing cars had softened halos, their glow hardly penetrating the swirling gray mist. *Fuck, this would make a good setting for a horror movie.* Landry grappled with the long pole he needed to pull down the rolling shutter. The metal hook on the end of the pole wasn't that big and Landry had to squint to see the hole he was supposed to get it through. He cursed as he missed for the third time. He wouldn't be much use at fending off a horror movie villain if he couldn't even manage to bring the shutters down.

"Do you need a hand with that?"

Landry jumped about a foot into the air and dropped the pole, which banged him on the temple then got tangled around his legs, bringing him to his knees.

"Fuck, fuck, fuck. And ow." He rubbed at his head. "Do you always sneak up on people like that?"

Gage loomed over him, grinning. "On your knees already. I knew you'd be glad to see me. And I didn't sneak, you weren't paying attention." He grabbed the pole, hooked the shutter the first time and pulled it down in one smooth motion.

"Typical." Landry scrambled to his feet. He padlocked the shutters. "I would have got it next time."

"Sure you would. I'll carry the pole for you — you're likely to brain someone with it. Probably yourself."

"I'm quite capable of holding my own pole, thank you very much." Landry made a grab for it.

"I'm sure you are." Gage snorted with laughter and Landry realized what he'd said. "You can give me a demonstration later." He kept hold of the pole.

"Oh my God. You're still in high school. There was me thinking I was the immature one."

"Sorry…" Gage could barely speak for laughing. "Are you ready to go out?"

"Do I look like I'm ready?" Landry stood in the middle of the sidewalk, hands on hips. "I finished work about two minutes ago."

"In this fog, I can't tell." Gage peered at him. "You are a bit dusty." He picked something from Landry's hair. "And you have a pet spider inhabiting your mop." He waved a few wisps of cobweb in Landry's direction.

Landry danced around, batting at his head. "Is it gone? Is it gone?"

"I never actually saw a spider…just cobwebs."

"You…you…" Landry stamped his foot. "You're unbelievable."

"And you're a brat." Gage gave him a swift smack on the ass. "Shower. I booked our table for nine."

Landry debated the wisdom of telling Gage to fuck off, but curiosity won out. His ass smarted from one blow and he wanted more of that. Gage was infuriating but intriguing. He didn't back off from Landry's attitude—in fact, it seemed to attract him more. "We have to go around back."

"I thought you'd finished work."

"I have, but I live up there." Landry pointed at the building. "Did that not come up in your background checks?"

"Probably… Must have missed that page of the report."

Gage, still carrying the pole, followed Landry down the side of the building. A gate in the boundary wall led to a small yard, stacked with terracotta pots of varying sizes. There was a barred door into the building between a pile of wooden crates and a plant of undetermined origin in a glazed urn.

"You should have more lighting back here. It's not safe."

"The only thing likely to jump me out here," Landry said, "is a rat. In this part of town, they grow to the size of wombats."

"Wombats?"

"Why not?"

"I don't think we have wombats in the US."

"Well, we should. They're cute. To get back to the point, I've never had a problem locking up. This area is safe-ish, and isn't it a bit too soon to be getting overprotective?"

"No."

"Oookay then." Landry unlocked the back door. Gage was so close behind him. He stumbled inside but Gage caught him, preventing a fall. "You can let go now."

"I don't think so." Gage put the pole in a corner then shoved Landry against the nearest wall, pushing a knee between his thighs, forcing his legs apart. He grabbed Landry's wrists, holding them together above his head. He kissed him and there was nothing Landry could, or wanted, to do to stop him. Gage tasted of coffee. His stubble scraped Landry's face as he probed with his tongue, gripping Landry's hair so he couldn't move. Finally, Gage let go and Landry took a couple of deep, shuddering breaths.

"I thought I should say hello properly."

Landry distracted himself by locking the door. The best kiss he'd ever experienced had left him shaken and uncertain. Part of him wanted to drag Gage up the stairs so they could make use of a convenient flat surface — another part wanted to run. "You should know, I don't put out on a first date." He stomped up the stairs.

"Well, it's good that this is our second date then."

"How do you work that out?" Landry stripped off his sweaty T-shirt as soon as he got inside his apartment, heading for the bathroom.

"I bought you coffee and baked goods yesterday. That constitutes a date."

"And where is that written, *Gage's Guide to Dating*? Um...I don't need your help to get clean, thank you." Landry tried to shut the door but Gage stuck a foot in the way.

"You're already flaunting your hot little bod. I think I should get to see the rest of it."

"Out." Landry scowled. "Or do I need to use my safe word already?"

"Good to know you have one." Gage grinned but withdrew his foot. Landry slammed the door shut, wishing he could lock it, but he'd never bothered to fit a bolt. He stripped off the rest of his clothes, dumped them in the hamper then dove behind the shower curtain, just in case. That meant he couldn't escape the cold spray from the shower. Usually he had to wait a few minutes for the cranky plumbing to produce hot water. He yelped.

"You okay in there?" Gage sounded smug.

Landry gritted his teeth, picturing Gage leaning against the wall right outside the bathroom. "I'm fine. Go make yourself a drink or something. You're upsetting my equilibrium. I'm sure you can find the kitchen, and work out what lives where, on your own."

Gage's laughter faded as he headed away. Landry tilted his head back, letting the spray batter his face.

What the hell am I getting myself into? He gripped his rigid cock. *And you're so not helping.* He braced himself against the chipped tile. A few quick tugs and Landry sank his teeth into his lower lip to stop himself from shouting as he came in a thigh-trembling gush of relief and euphoria. He clenched his ass muscles, craving the pressure of a thick cock lodged in his passage. He wondered if Gage was big everywhere. *God, I hope so.*

"Landry, you are such a slut." After a few deep, cleansing breaths, Landry summoned the will to apply shampoo and shower gel. He rinsed, turned off the water then shook his head like a soggy Labrador. Groping for a towel, he realized he hadn't brought fresh clothes in with him, which meant either putting his dirty things back on or making a run for his bedroom. After giving his dripping hair a vigorous rub, he opted for the latter. Gripping the corners of his towel tight, he pushed the door open a crack. There was no sign of Gage so he shimmied around the door then tiptoed toward his bedroom, just a few feet away.

"You have good coffee."

"Fuck!" Landry whirled around to find Gage lounging in the kitchen doorway, smirking, a steaming mug in his hand. "I'm glad you like it." He gripped his towel so tight his knuckles ached.

"You want one?"

"Oh God, yes."

"Then drop the towel."

"What? No!"

"It's a fair exchange. Coffee for the towel." Gage inhaled over his mug, then sighed. "So good."

"You're...you're...infuriating."

"And *you* are stunning."

Heat built in Landry's cheeks. Cursing, he shoved open his bedroom door with one hip, sidled into the room then slammed it shut. He wasn't used to feeling so off balance. He had been seconds away from doing exactly as Gage ordered and not because he wanted coffee that much. Gage was unpredictable, exciting, and Landry's fight or flight instincts were warring with each other. Gage made his desires clear but things were moving too fast for Landry. This was different from a casual hook-up—he wanted it to be more. Gage appealed to him in a way he hadn't experienced before and it scared him.

"Well, he's not going to get everything his own way." Landry pulled open the double doors of his art deco wardrobe. It was a gorgeous piece but a few bits of the veneer had peeled away so Mr. Lao had consigned it to Landry's apartment rather than putting it up for sale. He shoved hangers around, trying to decide what to wear. Other than telling him they were going out to eat, Gage hadn't given him any details about the restaurant. For all Landry knew, they could have a nine 'o clock reservation at the hot dog stand near the park. He fingered the fabric of his only pair of leather pants but decided against them in favor of a fresh pair of black, skinny jeans—this time with no tears. A fitted, light blue shirt, which had been a gift from his mother, completed the ensemble. *Conservatively sexy, if there is such a thing.* He pulled on socks and a pair of black Vans that he'd found in a thrift store, brand-new, still in the box. Something he'd credited to the influence of a new lucky cat he'd acquired the same day.

He ran his fingers through his hair, which never achieved any kind of style, then added a little kohl around his eyes and a slick of clear lip gloss. As ready as he would ever be, Landry made his way through to the kitchen where he found Gage leaning against the units, drinking the last of his coffee and looking completely at home. Landry accepted the mug Gage handed him then took his time examining him from head to toe. The man cleaned up well. The fine-knit sweater he wore hugged every curve of his body. His jeans, black like Landry's, gripped his thighs and the curve of his ass. He had long legs, currently crossed at the ankles to display heavy boots that added an inch to his height. Landry caught the scent of lemons behind the aroma of coffee and breathed deeply.

"Like what you see?" Gage was grinning.

Landry shrugged. "Maybe I like a man for his mind rather than the way he looks." He took several deep swallows of coffee, draining the mug in seconds. "Where are we going?"

"It's a surprise. You'll have to wait and see, but not for long because we need to leave if we're going to get there for nine. It's a short drive." Gage walked over to him and Landry took an involuntary step back but it was a small room and there was nowhere for him to go. Gage crowded against him. He stroked the side of Landry's neck then gave his earlobe a gentle nip. "You look good."

The whispered words and hot breath so close to Landry's ear made him shiver and his cock plumped in the confines of his jeans. Gage cupped the bulge. "I have something for you." He pressed a ring of thick black rubber into Landry's hand. "I'll allow you to put this on yourself tonight, but just this once. In the future, that job will be mine."

"You want me to wear a cock ring?"

"No, it's not a request. I'm ordering you to wear it. I'm going to keep you hard and wanting all night."

"I…"

"The appropriate response is 'Yes, Sir'."

"You can't... I mean, I won't..."

"Landry, go to the bathroom, put the ring on."

Landry gave a strangled whimper. "Fine... Sir."

"On any other night that tone would get you a spanking. Now do as you're told, or we'll be late."

Landry scampered back to the bathroom, slamming the door behind him in the only gesture of defiance he could manage. Gage's commands had made him painfully hard. He tore open his jeans then fitted the tight rubber ring around the base of his cock, not easy in his current state. There was no way he wanted to come in his pants like a teenager while he was out on a date so he told himself that obeying was practical. Acceptance didn't make his balls ache any less or make it easier to get his stiff cock back into his jeans. He zipped up with great care, wondering whether going commando had been such a good idea. He yanked on the hem of his shirt, hoping it was long enough to cover his embarrassment.

"Fuckety fuck. Should have worn looser pants." The outline of his cock beneath the soft denim was clear for anyone to see. The bathroom door swung open.

"That's long enough, let's go." Gage took a firm hold of Landry's wrist then towed him toward the front door. Unresisting, Landry allowed him to lead the way.

"Are you going to act like a caveman all night?"

"Act?" Gage blinked then shrugged. "Pretty much. Any objections?"

Landry was focused on not tripping down the stairs but he couldn't think of a single good reason for Gage to behave differently. He kept his silence, wondering how this date would turn out. He had an idea that Gage's plan for a good night wouldn't fit social norms. Landry wasn't the black sheep of his family — more like the kinky rainbow lamb everyone wanted to protect —

but he'd never considered himself normal, whatever that was. *Bring it on, Detective.* The night promised to be the start of a great new adventure.

Chapter Four

Gage kept his hand on the small of Landry's back all the way to his parking spot. There was something about the man that made Gage want to touch. He wondered how much wriggling it had taken Landry to get into his pants because they could have been spray-painted on. Not that Gage objected, far from it, but it might have been fun to watch the squirming, especially as he was sure there could be no room for underwear beneath the denim.

"Which one is your ride?" Landry asked, scanning the parked vehicles. "No, don't tell me. It's the Lexus."

"How much do you think detectives bring in?"

"Not the Prius? Please no, I have to maintain a modicum of street cred." Landry bounced on his toes.

"Try the other side of the street, smart ass."

"Oh my God, it's the beaten-up Jeep, isn't it?" Landry jogged across the street without checking for traffic. "Have you been off-roading in this thing? Because I've seen less muck on the speedway track after three straight days of rain."

"It's camouflage." Gage yanked open the passenger door. "Get in, and did no one ever tell you to look both ways before crossing the street?" He waited until Landry was safely inside the Jeep before circling the vehicle to get behind the wheel.

"It's scary clean in here." Landry put on his seat belt. "I was expecting Krispy Kreme boxes, take-out cups, burger wrappers..." He swiped a finger along the dash as if checking for dust. "Did you get it valeted just for me?"

"No, I did not. I spend more time in this car than I do at the station. I don't like living in a pigsty."

"Smells...lemony." Landry prodded various buttons.

"Maybe one day I'll get you to wash it." Gage slapped Landry's wandering hand away from the CD player before turning on the ignition. "Naked."

"That doesn't sound like fun...though there are advantages to getting wet and sudsy. It's comfy in here. I like it." Landry tugged at the glove compartment. "Locked. My bad."

"I'm a cop. What do you expect to find in there?" Gage kept his eyes on the road.

"Uh, dunno...donuts or a first aid kit? Oh my God! Is it locked because you have a freakin' gun in there?"

"It's a spare, and why do you have an obsession with cops and donuts?"

"Don't tell me it's an urban myth because that will destroy me."

Gage thought about some of his colleagues. "Nah, it's true. Most of the cops I know run on adrenaline, caffeine and sugar."

"But not you?"

"I have been known to indulge in the occasional chocolate custard, though why I'm admitting that to you I've no idea."

"You're making me hungry and I'm good at making people talk. They seem to open up to me. No idea why."

"Because they want to get a word in edgewise? I need to invest in a whole new set of gags." Gage sighed. "So what do you drive?"

"Does a skateboard count?" Landry nibbled a fingernail.

"Stop that or I'll tie your hands behind your back."

Landry shoved his hands under his thighs. "No fair."

"So, do you have a license or did someone with sense decide you'd be a liability behind the wheel?"

"Hey! I can drive but I'd much rather be a passenger. Traffic in Seattle is super scary and people yell at me when I miss a green light because there's a good song on the radio."

Gage tried to keep up but decided to give it up as a lost cause. He drove the next five minutes half listening to Landry's running commentary on everything they passed. "We're here. Pray for a parking space."

"There, by the dumpster!"

"Nice spot." Gage reversed the car into a space he would probably have missed. He switched off the ignition then turned to Landry. "I should tell you that the restaurant we're going to is a bit different. It's called The Bowline."

Landry gaped. "You're kidding me! That place is impossible to get a table at. I've always wanted to go there because everyone at the club talks about it."

"Which club do you go to?" Gage asked.

"I have a membership at Scorch."

"Good choice. It's the safest option in this city."

"I know. I've been to a few others on open nights but the owners at Scorch are good guys—they vet everyone, and subs get really low membership rates. Are we really going to The Bowline? 'Cause if we are I might let you get to second base tonight."

"Yes, we are and I want you on your best behavior. The owners are friends of mine."

"Yes, Sir." For once there wasn't a trace of sarcasm in Landry's tone. There was a touch of awe.

Mitch opened the door to the restaurant before Gage reached for the bell.

"Welcome to The Bowline!" He ushered them inside. "Good to see you, Gage, and this is…?"

"Landry, meet Mitchell Alvarez-Cross, wine connoisseur and general gopher around this place while his husband, Diego, works his magic in the kitchen."

"It's a pleasure to meet you. Really. I can't believe I'm here." Landry stared, wide-eyed, at everything.

"Seems your reputation precedes you," Gage said, amused.

"And so it should." Mitch grinned. "Let me show you to your table."

Gage followed Mitch across the restaurant, weaving between tables occupied by a mix of couples and small groups. A naked sub was laid across one table, his Dom feasting from an array of chopped fruit spread over his body. At another, a Dom sat alone but from the blissful expression on his face, Gage guessed the floor-length cloth concealed more than table legs. Two couples occupied a table inside a cage—both subs had collars attached to the bars by long chains.

"Wow. Oh, wow." Landry tripped but Gage caught him before he fell.

"You need to watch where you're going," Gage scolded, enjoying the warmth of Landry's body in his arms.

"But, there's so much to see!" Landry pouted.

"And you're welcome to look, young man," Mitch said. "Guests wanting privacy choose the booths or concealed tables. Everyone else expects to be seen — it's part of their fun. Takes all sorts."

"My friends at Scorch are gonna be the same color as Shrek when I tell them I've been here."

Gage shook his head. "This isn't about making your friends jealous. It's about having a nice night out in surroundings where we can be ourselves and where the food tops any upscale restaurant in the city."

"Uh-huh. That too. They're still gonna be green as Kermit."

Mitch gestured to a staircase leading to a raised platform. "Your table is up there. Go settle in. Menus are on the table. I'll bring some iced water in a few minutes."

"Thanks, Mitch. I'll have to send a fruit basket to Ben and Carl."

"I've reserved the same table for them in four weeks' time. Carl should be all fixed by then."

"Then I don't feel quite so bad." Gage climbed the stairs, following Landry, who'd already disappeared behind the thick velvet drapes. The hidden table was lit by a series of lanterns slung around the curtain rail, making the atmosphere romantic but cozy. It wasn't so dark that they'd have to squint to see their food.

"This is amazing!" Landry sat on one of the plush chairs, bouncing to test its comfort. "So far you're scoring major date points, and I have exacting standards."

"Oh, you do, do you?" Gage took the chair next to him, rather than sitting opposite.

"Of course. You can tell a lot about a prospective boyfriend from his approach to a date. A hot dog after a bad movie signals a definite lack of commitment. Splashing the cash is all about getting into my pants, but marks me down as shallow and easily impressed, which I'm not."

"I'm glad I meet the bar," Gage said, trying not to laugh.

"So far… It's not a sure thing until the end of the night." Landry picked up the menu. "How am I expected to choose? This all sounds so good." He wrinkled his nose in apparent concentration, the tip of his tongue poked between his lips.

"Do you have any strong likes or dislikes?" Gage asked.

"I'll eat anything," Landry said. "Except snails because even garlic butter can't redeem them. Or baby octopus because they're far too cute to be eaten."

"Noted. I can order for us both."

"Okay."

"No arguments? I expected more resistance."

"If we want to eat tonight, it's best you choose. I'll be dithering over my choices for hours."

"Indecisive, huh?"

"Like you wouldn't believe. The only reason I can decide what to have for breakfast is because I only keep one box of cereal in the kitchen."

"Let me guess, Lucky Charms?"

"How did you know?"

"Detective, remember?"

"Were you poking around my kitchen cupboards earlier?"

"No comment."

When Mitch reappeared to take their order, Gage chose an easy starter to share, avoiding garlic. For the main course he opted for Diego's specialty, which was a sampler of dishes.

"Food will be about fifteen minutes, so what about drinks?"

"Just the iced water for me," Gage said. "I'm driving."

"Same," Landry said. "I get tipsy if I so much as sniff alcohol. One drink and my inhibitions take a vacation to Honolulu, complete with Hawaiian shirt."

Mitch grinned. "Water it is." He left, returning a few minutes later with a large pitcher and two glasses. "Enjoy. Diego says hi but he's up to his ears in cooking."

"Say hi back," Gage said. "You guys will have to come round to my place for dinner soon."

"Only if Diego brings the ingredients and cooks in your kitchen," Mitch said. "Your last attempt was disastrous."

Gage shrugged. "Why do you think I'm inviting you over? That was a one-off. I need to redeem myself and prove my skills."

Landry giggled and shared a smile with Mitch.

"No ganging up on me, you two. That one time I was a bit too ambitious, but I love to experiment. I don't have time to practice much, is all. My mac and cheese is sublime and besides, diners would cease to exist if it weren't for people like me."

"So it's a public service you're providing?" Mitch headed down the steps before Gage could respond.

"And *you*, giggle boy, are digging yourself into a hole that you'll need a ladder to get out of."

Landry fiddled with a napkin. "Am I in trouble?"

"I get the feeling you're in trouble most of the time," Gage said.

"I think I should be offended, but Mr. Lao calls me a trouble magnet so I can't deny it. I just seem to fall into situations… They're never my fault."

"Right. Of course they're not."

Before Gage could say anything further, Mitch returned with a basket of flatbread and a dish of oil before rushing off again.

"He's gonna get a lot of exercise going up and down those steps tonight," Landry said.

"He runs marathons for fun. I don't think a few steps bother him much." Gage leaned back in his seat. "So, apart from going to Scorch, what do you do for fun?"

"Between Treasure Trove and the club, I don't have much free time," Landry said. "I like browsing the street markets and window-shopping. I don't go to a gym because I get enough exercise walking everywhere and carrying stuff in the store." He patted his flat belly. "I'm lucky I can eat what I want and never gain a pound. What about you, what do you do other than solve crimes and eat donuts?"

"Well, I do admit to going to the gym at the station every now and again but I like getting out to the national parks, or into the mountains. My sister has an RV that she lets me take out whenever she's not using it. I like to park somewhere wild, hike a little, take photographs, just sit and read."

"Sounds cool. Other than summer camp when I was a kid, I haven't traveled much at all. Have you ever seen a bear or a moose, oh, or a wolf?"

"All three over the years, lots of other critters too. I like the peace of being on my own."

Landry sipped his water, wetting his lips to a shade of dark red. A drop escaped and trickled down his chin. "Don't you get lonely?"

"I like my own company," Gage admitted. "Though sometimes I think it would be nice to have someone to share the privacy with." Something in his expression must have triggered a response in Landry because he blushed, the pink on his cheeks visible even in the dim light.

"What were you just thinking about?" Gage asked.

"Um… I think it's a bit early in the evening to be talking about my fantasies, don't you?"

Gage shrugged. "I can just torture it out of you later." He watched Landry's pretty lips form an 'O' shape. It took a lot of effort to keep a straight face. "See the chair next to you? Take a closer look at the seat."

Landry prodded at the cushion until he discovered the swivel mechanism. The entire seat flipped over to reveal a rubber dildo fixed to the wooden surface. "Oh my…"

"A nice accompaniment to the dessert course."

Landry gulped. "I don't think I could…"

"But it won't be your choice, will it?"

"No, Sir." Landry's gaze was firmly fixed to the dildo.

"Look at me, Landry." Gage gave him a few seconds then tilted his chin up. "I'll never ask you to do anything you don't want to. I know you have a safe word and I expect you to use it if you need to, especially while we're getting to know each other. I have no idea of your boundaries yet, and though I'm not averse to pushing you over them, I don't get off on scaring people."

The tension disappeared from Landry's shoulders. "I'm glad. But I wasn't scared."

"No?"

"Nope. Turned on *waaaay* too much." Landry slipped a hand under the table.

"Are you touching something you shouldn't?"

"No, Sir? I mean, I am touching something and it feels really nice in a frustrating, this-cock-ring-is-too-tight kind of way, but you didn't say I couldn't, so..."

"Stop touching, Landry. That pout won't get you anywhere with me." Landry's lip jutted even further but he put his hands on the table.

"So we're clear, what is your safe word?"

"Words. Ming Dynasty."

Gage stared at him. "I got nothing. I'm afraid to ask..."

"Because ancient porcelain is fragile and sensitive to extreme conditions. Like me."

"You. Fragile. Not my first impression."

"I'm fragile when my ass is getting whipped. I'm not into extreme pain."

"Me either. Though a good paddling or spanking can be satisfying for all involved."

Landry's eyes got a bit glazed and he licked his lips.

"Focus, Landry."

"What? Oh, sorry...I zoned out there a little, didn't I? When you say things like that, my balls get bluer. I'm guessing powder blue at the moment."

"Plenty of shades to get through yet then. Oh great, here's our first course."

Landry's fidgeting made Gage smile. He'd have a quiet word with Mitch and request some restraints for later. Stiff leather ones.

Chapter Five

Landry dipped a piece of flatbread into a dish of oil. As he ate it, the oil coated his lips. "Mmm, this is good stuff. I'm no expert, but I can tell high-quality virgin olive oil when I taste it."

Gage brushed a crumb of bread from the corner of Landry's mouth. "The starter is even better. King prawns fried in Diego's secret recipe batter, served with sweet chili sauce, hot enough to make your lips sting."

"That sounds fantastic. I adore seafood." Landry reached for a prawn, only to have his hand slapped away. Gage picked one up instead, dipped it in the translucent red sauce then held it to Landry's lips. Landry hesitated a second before taking a bite. He wasn't sure how he felt about being fed, but the delicate batter melted on his tongue and the succulent prawn beneath dissolved any reservations he might have had. A second or two later, the chili sauce hit his taste buds, leaving fire in its wake. "Wow!" He parted his lips like a baby bird asking for more and Gage obliged, feeding him several prawns before taking any for himself.

"Those were a great choice." Landry took a few swallows of water. He prodded the pile of cast-off prawn tails. "Oh, they're all gone."

"You need to keep some room for the main course," Gage said, smiling. "I do like a man with healthy appetites."

"Are we still talking about food here, or did you just pluralize by mistake?"

"I don't know, are we?"

Landry shivered. Gage affected him in a way he hadn't experienced before. A word, his tone, a glance… Each was capable of dissolving Landry's brain cells and sending all his blood rushing south. It was frightening in a nerve-tingling, exciting way. For once, he had no idea what to say.

"Let's enjoy the food for now," Gage said, as Mitch arrived with the next course. He cleared the used dishes and left finger bowls of warm water, which Gage made use of. There was an assortment of plates, each heaped with fragrant selections. Landry identified two kinds of fish, a chicken dish and something made with a mixture of wild mushrooms. Everything looked fantastic and he didn't know where to start. He waited, wondering if Gage would insist on feeding him again, but Gage handed him a fork.

"Dig in. I thought the tasting menu would suit us as I didn't know what your favorites might be. These are all Diego's specialties and I can recommend every single one of them. Try them all or he'll be upset."

"Which one is your favorite?"

"All of them." Gage's fork hovered over the chicken dish. "But if I had to pick, then this one would probably edge out the others. It has saffron in it and I don't know how he does it, but Diego manages to flavor the rice to perfection. I'd like to have a go at recreating the recipe but he won't tell me the secret ingredients."

"And there was me thinking detectives were trained in interrogation techniques." Landry took a forkful of the chicken and chewed slowly. He moaned. "Oh my God, this is miraculous."

"We are. But as Mitch will happily tell you, Diego's more stubborn than a cranky mule."

Landry shrugged. "To be honest, I don't care what's in it. I just want to eat it." He dug in, intent on tasting all the dishes. Communication was reduced to vague, orgasmic mumblings. There wasn't anything he didn't like and between them, he and Gage cleared every plate. Landry sat back in his seat, rubbing his belly. "My stomach thinks I've died and gone to heaven. Thank you for bringing me here, Gage. It's a special place and it means a lot that you shared it with me."

"Maybe I think you're worth it," Gage mumbled.

"Did you just pay me a sort of compliment?" Landry asked, trying not to laugh. Gage apparently fulfilled every male stereotype when it came to voicing his feelings.

"Absolutely not. Do you have room for dessert?"

"If the sweets are as good as the other courses were, I'll fit one in. Besides, I'll save on groceries because I'm not gonna need to eat for the rest of the week."

The curtains rustled and, right on cue, Mitch appeared. "I thought you guys might be about ready for me to clear. For dessert, we have a choice of bitter chocolate mousse with mint chocolate spears, cherry pie with home-made vanilla ice cream or Eton mess, which is British and from what I can tell, consists of smashed meringue, fruit and enormous quantities of whipped cream. I'm hoping there will be some of that left over for me."

"We'll take the chocolate mousse," Gage said before whispering something Landry couldn't quite catch into Mitch's ear. Mitch grinned before making his way back down the stairs.

"How did you know the mousse would be my favorite?" Landry asked.

"Detective, remember?"

"You use that line a lot, don't you?"

"It comes in handy."

Landry was getting fidgety. His dick ached and Gage's growly tones weren't helping him control his libido. A home run was getting more and more likely. Landry clenched his ass muscles. It had been far too long since he'd been filled with anything other than a plug and he'd bet a few dollars that Gage was in proportion in all the right places.

"What are you thinking about?" Gage interrupted his daydreams. "Your eyes got all glazed for a minute there."

"Mousse?" There was no way Landry was going to admit to his actual thoughts.

"Bullshit. I'll let it slide for now…but I will find out what's going on in that pretty head of yours."

"Patronizing much? Wait…you think I'm pretty?" Landry nibbled on his lower lip.

"I think you need a damn good spanking. That's what *I* was thinking about."

That made Landry fidget even more. "You're very forward for a first date."

"Second date, and I don't see the point in obfuscation."

Landry gaped. "Did you swallow a dictionary along with the main course?"

"I like to do crossword puzzles on stakeouts. It passes the time."

Landry fiddled with his napkin. It seemed Gage was a man of many layers and a smart remark didn't feel appropriate. The curtain swung aside and Mitch appeared carrying a glass bowl heaped with mousse studded with the promised mint chocolate spears. Landry's mouth watered. There wasn't much he wouldn't do for chocolate. Mitch placed the bowl on the table. Next to it he laid two sets of handcuffs. He gave Landry a wink before retreating down the stairs.

Landry eyed Gage. "What are you intending to do with those?"

"Well they aren't for using on me." Gage rose from his seat and grabbed the cuffs. He locked one bracelet of each set around the bars on either side of Landry's head. Lifting Landry's right arm, Gage slipped a cuff around Landry's wrist. He gave him ample opportunity to resist but Landry remained passive.

"My mom always said my curiosity would get me into trouble one day," Landry whined. Gage imprisoned his other wrist and Landry gave an experimental tug on the cuffs.

"She was right. That's much better." Gage shifted the table to one side of the booth, leaving a clear space in front of Landry's legs. He put the bowl of mousse on the floor before sinking to his knees. Landry's heart pounded. *It's not possible that he's going to do what I'm imagining, is it? Doms don't get on their knees and they don't...* His thoughts were interrupted by the lowering of his zipper and Gage's wicked, wicked grin. Landry's ringed cock sprang to attention, bobbing with sheer joy at the unexpected freedom. *A few tugs is all I need...* Landry yanked on the cuffs but his hands were closer to his ears than his cock. He moaned in frustration. Humping the seat didn't help, nor did squeezing his thighs together. Gage watched him struggle, smirking.

"You're evil." Landry scowled but when Gage presented a spoonful of mousse to his lips, he opened obediently. "Oh, that's...more, please!" Gage fed him until more than half the bowl had disappeared, then he used the spoon to smear a dollop over the head of Landry's cock. Stunned, Landry could do nothing but watch as Gage licked him from root to tip, gathering the decadent mousse onto his tongue.

"Mmm. Tasty."

"Oh my God!" Landry's cock jerked.

"This may take a while." Gage took his own sweet time working his way through the rest of the dessert, scooping, licking and sucking until Landry had tears rolling down his face.

"Please! Gage...Sir!"

Despite Landry's increasingly desperate begging, Gage didn't relent until all the mousse was gone. Then he eased the ring from the base of Landry's cock.

"You have a choice."

"You want a conversation now?"

"Evil, remember? Now pay attention. Three options. One—I put the cock ring back on and you don't get to come until I drop you off at home later."

Landry whimpered. "So evil."

"Option two—my hand. On condition that our next date happens at the club and I give you a public spanking. Or option three—my mouth, but tomorrow I lock your pretty dick in a cock cage, which doesn't come off until our next date." Gage rubbed his thumb over the head of Landry's weeping cock. "One, two or three, Landry. Take too long and I'll choose for you."

Landry had no doubt Gage meant every word. He also knew there was no way he could wait until he got home. He had to come. It was imperative. He weighed the other options as best he could, considering ninety-nine percent of his attention was on his aching balls. "Three! You're an utter bastard, you know that, don't you?"

Gage plunged his mouth over Landry's shaft, taking his whole length without hesitation. Landry's cock hit the back of Gage's throat and Gage swallowed. Landry screamed, yanking on both set of handcuffs, the metal digging into his wrists. Gage sucked, letting his teeth scrape the smallest amount. Landry threw back his head, his orgasm intense and overwhelming. He sobbed through several full-body shudders, spurting into Gage's mouth. When he was done, Gage licked his lips then got to his feet.

"Delicious." He released the handcuffs before drawing Landry onto his lap, holding him close. "You're shaking."

"You think?"

Gage chuckled. "Still a brat." He tucked Landry's cock into his pants. Landry did the zipper himself.

"What about you, Gage? I'm not some selfish, self-obsessed princess. I can…"

"You can sit there and stop talking. Pretty sure Mitch will have a nice selection of gags and there's bound to be one I like."

"You're unbelievable." Landry snuggled against Gage's chest. He patted a pec. "Could do with a bit more cushioning for optimum comfort, but muscles work for me too."

"I'm so glad."

"Um, you're vibrating."

"Fuck. That's my phone." Gage groped in his pocket, nudging Landry's rear as he did.

"Stop feeling me up."

"Hey, I can multi-task." Gage dragged his phone out. "Roskam." He listened for a few seconds. "Well, fuck. I'll be there in thirty." He disconnected.

"I guess our date is over," Landry said.

"Sorry but yes. I'll take you home on the way."

"Hazard of dating a cop, I suppose." Landry nuzzled Gage's neck, breathing in his scent. "I was so gonna put out for you." He patted Gage's bulging crotch. "Is this uncomfortable?"

"You little…" Gage hoisted Landry off his lap. "Just you wait until tomorrow."

Landry gulped. He should know better than to play with matches near flammable material. "I can get a cab home if it's easier."

"No."

"No?"

"No." Gage pushed aside the curtain around their booth then led Landry down the stairs. He waved Mitch over. "We gotta run, buddy. I got called in. Thanks for a fantastic meal. You'll tell Diego?"

"Sure I will." Mitch waved away Gage's credit card. "I know where you live. Call in next time you're passing and not in a rush to be somewhere else. You can pay then. I have hungry kinksters to feed. It was great to meet you, Landry. Don't let this big lug intimidate you. He's a kitty cat under that rough exterior."

Landry grinned. "I won't."

"Less of the 'rough', please." Gage manhandled Landry toward the door. "And stop making puppy eyes at the other diners, brat."

"I wasn't!" Landry protested. "Though there are some super-hawt guys in here now you mention it."

"I didn't mention it. Out!" They were followed by snorts of laughter and applause. "One night with you and my reputation is ruined," Gage grumbled, but he still put his arm around Landry's shoulders as they walked back to the Jeep.

Landry settled into his seat with a sigh of contentment. "You're going to have to work hard to beat that when it comes to our next date. The food was incredible and the setting was perfect. Dessert was sublime. Thank you."

"I wish we could take the evening to a much more interesting conclusion."

Landry wasn't ready for the night to end either but he could be a grown-up. "It sucks big hairy donkey balls that you have to go but I would never get between you and your job. Just don't get dead while you're doing it."

"Is that an order?" Gage sounded amused.

Landry thought about it. "Yes. Because it wouldn't be fair."

"On you?"

"No, on you, because you would never have had the chance to get up close and personal with my exceptionally cute butt and that would be tragic." He ignored Gage's exasperated sigh. "Are you allowed to tell me where you're going or is it all secret squirrel stuff?"

"Secret what?"

"Squirrel. You know, small, furry, big fluffy tail, comes in red and gray varieties."

"I know what a squirrel is."

"But you don't watch cartoons?"

"Not since my balls dropped, no."

"*Secret Squirrel* is one of my favorites. I like *Hong Kong Phooey* too. I could introduce you to grown-up stuff as well. Have you ever seen *Archer*?"

"I don't watch much TV and how did we get here? Navigating your conversation is like finding my way around a maize maze."

"Ooh, have you ever done one of those? I think it would be romantic to get lost together then find the middle and indulge in some celebratory kissing. So long as the walls don't move. Have you seen *Harry Potter*? Tell me you have. Oh my God, you haven't! There's a scene in a maze...never mind, what about *Labyrinth*? David Bowie in long boots and really tight pants?"

"No idea what you're talking about."

"I think I'm going to cry."

"Then our next date should be on your sofa and you can educate me in the ways of maze-related films." Gage swung into a space at the front of Treasure Trove. "I'll walk you in."

"There's no need." Landry scrambled out of the Jeep. Gage was right behind him and even though Landry had said not to bother, Gage's overprotectiveness made Landry's insides go squishy. He unlocked the door before turning into Gage's arms.

"Be good, brat. I'll be in touch."

"I'm not working tomorrow so if you want to catch that film..."

"I'll call you. Don't know how things will pan out with the case yet."

"Okay." Landry moaned into the kiss that followed. Gage groped Landry's ass.

"And don't forget the choice you made at the restaurant."

"You meant that?" Landry gulped. Gage treated him to a far more chaste kiss before stepping away.

"I meant it." Then he was gone, leaving Landry to deal with another erection and a mild sense of panicked anticipation.

Chapter Six

On Sundays, Landry had a routine. A long morning spent lounging in bed with coffee and a book before facing the day. He liked to clean the apartment and do laundry before taking a shower around lunchtime, and he didn't feel guilty about keeping the afternoon for himself. Today was different because Mr. Lao was heading for the airport and Landry helped carry his suitcase out to the sidewalk. He felt it wise to put on pants in order to accomplish the task without getting arrested and that alone was enough to upset his day.

"You'll lock up properly every night while I'm gone?" Mr. Lao asked for the third time.

"Yessir. Cash in the safe at the end of the day until the secure courier comes at the end of the week. No wine, women or hanky-panky on the shop floor."

Mr. Lao gave him a cuff around the ear. "No wine, *men* or hanky-panky. I didn't come down in the last shower — no creating loopholes in the rules."

Landry grinned. "It was worth a try. Here's your cab."

"No need to sound so joyful you're getting rid of me." Mr. Lao got into the back of the cab while Landry manhandled his case into the trunk.

"I'll miss you, Mr. L.," Landry said. It was the truth. He got on well with the old man and was more than a little anxious about being left in sole charge of the shop.

Mr. Lao shut the cab door then wound down the window. "You'll be fine. You have good instincts. Any real problems, call my cousin Soong."

"He lives in Florida and he's eighty." Landry couldn't imagine Soong being much help in any kind of crisis.

"Don't be ageist, he's more agile than he looks. Seriously, he can mobilize the family if you need them."

"Have a great trip and try not to worry. I'll look forward to seeing all the goodies you bring back for the store."

Mr. Lao grunted then rolled up his window. As the cab pulled into the traffic, Landry headed around to the back of the building. There was a diner two blocks away that did a bargain breakfast and Landry had every intention of gorging himself while consuming several pots of coffee.

"It's far too early to be vertical," he muttered as he headed inside to fetch his wallet and phone. With the scent of coffee enticing him, Landry trotted the two blocks to the diner. Once inside, he waved to Basim, the owner, before making his way to a window booth. Landry liked to people watch over a stack of pancakes dripping with syrup. He didn't have to tell Basim his order and within ten minutes he had his pancakes and a side plate piled with crisp bacon strips. He got his own miniature jug of warm maple syrup. It was an indulgence reserved for Sundays, when he had time to eat at his leisure. Bacon was never to be hurried. That was the law. It was busy, so once he was done eating, Landry gave up his booth to a harried father wrangling six small boys in baseball uniforms. Landry took a seat at the counter, waiting for Basim to refill his coffee.

"Busy morning, Bas."

"Good business, Landry, my boy. Plenty of dollars coming my way." Basim grinned, revealing a gold tooth. Landry knew Basim sent money to his aging mother in Pakistan so he didn't begrudge him a cent. "You want more food? You need fattening up."

"Is that you or your ma speaking?" Landry asked. He'd Skyped with Basim's mother on occasion and though Basim had to translate, the theme was always the same. Landry was too thin, he needed more of Basim's cooking, a mild breeze would blow him into traffic. Mothers were the same the world over.

"What can I say? She lives to feed people. She thinks I, and everyone I know, are starving for the lack of her cooking."

"She knows you own a diner, right?"

"But she's not here supervising the cooking, therefore it can only be substandard." Basim twirled one end of his substantial mustache. "She and my youngest brother are coming to visit in the summer. You must call in. There will be a big feast, all the delicacies from Faisalabad." Basim smacked his lips together.

"Sounds yum," Landry said. "I'll be there."

"And you bring your young man with you."

"Ah, I don't have one of those... Well, I kinda did meet someone, but it's new. Not sure it'll last. Yet."

"Does he have a decent job? Good family?"

"He's a cop..."

"Good, good." Basim rubbed his hands together. "Cops are always hungry. Bring him here. I see my profits rising."

"Basim, you have no shame." Landry hopped off his stool.

"I am a proud capitalist, it is true."

"Well, in the interests of keeping you in the latest Nikes, Mr. Lao has gone on a trip. I'm looking after the shop on my own for a while, so would it be okay for me to order food? I know you don't usually do take out..."

"Say no more. You call and I'll send one of the girls along, no problem."

"Thanks, Basim! I really appreciate that. Mr. Lao said I can close for an hour at lunchtime, but if there are customers in the store I can't exactly throw them out."

"The customer is king... Or queen," Basim added, after getting a glare from one of his staff. He sighed. "I am a repressed male."

"You are no such thing!" Laughing, Landry put some bills on the counter before heading to the door. "Have a good day, Basim."

"That I will, my young friend. That I will."

Landry sauntered along the sidewalk, pausing to admire an oil slick rainbow shimmering on the asphalt. He snapped a quick picture on his phone. It made him smile and put a bit more bounce in his step even though a light drizzle had started up. As he passed the front of Treasure Trove, he glanced at the lock holding the shutter in place. There was no sign of tampering and he gave a satisfied nod as he rounded the corner to the rear entrance. Once inside he decided to check that everything was tidy and ready for opening on Monday morning, then he'd be able to relax for the rest of the day.

The shop was quiet. Landry wandered the aisles, breathing in the scent of old wood, leather and paper. He ran his hand over an eighteenth-century chest made of golden oak, the wood warm to his touch. He made a mental note to vacuum one of the bookcases, which he'd missed if the layer of fine dust on the shelves was anything to go by.

"Probably got distracted by a customer," he muttered. He locked the door between the shop and the rear of the building and was about to head upstairs to his apartment when he thought he heard scratching at the outside door. "I hope that's not a rat." He jerked the door open then yelped as a man crashed into him. Landry landed on his back in the hallway, banging his elbow as he fell. The other man landed on top of him.

"Get offa me!" Landry yelped. His assailant was heavy.

"Fuck, sorry." The man scrambled clear, then stood. He offered Landry a hand. Cursing, Landry took it and was hauled to his feet.

"Who the fuck are you and why are you...skulking at the door?"

"Skulking?" The man grinned.

Landry took in floppy blond hair, several shades darker than his own, and amused, hazel eyes. There was a resemblance to Rupert Penry-Jones, a British actor Landry had a crush on. *Yum.* "What would you call it?" Landry dusted himself off. Pain shot through his elbow. "Ow!"

"Did you hurt yourself?" Concern crossed the blond's handsome face.

"No I didn't hurt myself. I was an innocent bystander. You hurt me. You knocked me down, then squished me," Landry complained, rubbing his sore arm. "Now, who the hell are you?"

"James Ellery, at your service. Please accept my humblest apologies for my entrance."

"That accent…British. Why are you British?"

"Um, because I was born in Colchester, which is a small county town in Essex, England."

"Okay, I admit that was a dumb question. Let's get back to why you're here." Landry had to admit that James' lopsided smile was charming.

"I'm an investigator." James fumbled in the inside pocket of his jacket and pulled out a wallet. He flipped it open to reveal a photo ID. Landry stared at it.

"That's a terrible picture."

"It is," James agreed. "I look like I have jaundice, but then I'd lay odds that your passport photograph doesn't make you look like a runway model either."

"So you're a private investigator?" Landry wasn't going to mention that he didn't have a passport. "That means you're like Magnum, or Remington Steele."

"How much ancient TV do you watch?"

"Hey, they're classics. You still haven't told me what you're doing here, in my hallway, in Seattle."

"I was told you have great coffee here."

"That's it, get out." Landry attempted to shove James out of the door but the investigator had at least eight inches on him and quite a few pounds. He didn't budge.

"Sorry, again. We've only just met and I've spent far too much time apologizing to you. Yes, I'm a private investigator but I work for insurance companies. I'm investigating the theft of some valuable jewelry and the trail has led me here."

"Not you too," Landry muttered.

"I arrived in the city last night and I've been checking out a few places. Today, I'm just getting my bearings because all the antique shops seem to be closed. I saw you come in here and I thought I'd introduce myself. Get ahead of the game, as it were."

"I don't know anything," Landry said. "I just work here, I don't own the place."

"Then perhaps you could introduce me to the owner?"

Landry wasn't about to give information on Mr. Lao's whereabouts to a complete stranger. "If you come back when the store's open tomorrow, I'd be happy to answer any questions you have."

"We could go for a coffee. I'm buying. I have a great expense account."

"I don't want to be rude, but this is my only day off all week and I have plans." Somehow, James had edged further into the hallway.

James blinked, then turned. "There's somebody coming."

"Landry, I thought I warned you about security. The street gate was open. Am I going to have to tan your hide?" Gage stood in the doorway, blocking the daylight. "Who is this?" He didn't sound pleased.

"James Ellery. Landry and I were just negotiating a first date." James turned to face Gage. "Pleased to meet you."

"We were not!" Landry said. "Gage, this guy showed up at the door. He says he's some kind of investigator but he's clingier than gum on my shoe. I've tried to be polite, but he won't leave."

James gave him a disarming smile. "Hey, I know when I've outstayed my welcome. Thanks for the invitation for tomorrow. I'll see you then." He slipped past Gage into the yard then was gone.

Gage stepped into the hallway. "I know we just met, Landry, but…"

"It's not what it looked like," Landry protested. "Not at all." He wrapped his arms around himself. "I'm glad you arrived because he was starting to scare me. Really. I couldn't get rid of him. He showed me some ID and told me he was an investigator for an insurance company looking into missing jewelry. He wanted to ask me questions and he was very persistent."

"Come here." Gage held his arms open and Landry walked into them. "I'm sorry I misinterpreted the situation. I'm kind of possessive."

Landry nuzzled against Gage's chest. "Just a tad."

"He sounded British."

"He was. Is. From Colchester. I don't know where that is."

"I'll check him out, make sure he is who he says he is."

"I'd appreciate that. He's probably going to show up again tomorrow." Landry extricated himself from Gage's hold. "Are you working?"

"No. I'm here for our next date. I brought snacks. Enough for some serious film viewing. That's if you're still up for it, of course. Though that's possibly not the best choice of phrases because you're not going to be up for anything for a while." Gage smirked.

"What do you have in that bag?" Landry asked.

"Chocolate popcorn, Twinkies, Cheetos, macadamia cookies and a pretty, stainless steel chastity tube."

"I…" Landry thought he might have a chance of making a run for it. If he were quick. Then Gage pushed the door shut with his ass.

"It was your choice."

"The snacks sound good."

"Are you going to lead the way to your apartment, or do I have to throw you over my shoulder and carry you up there?"

Landry sighed. "I'm on the top floor, remember? There's no elevator."

Gage shrugged. "I can caveman with the best of them."

"I'm sure. But no carrying. I just ate and you don't need me barfing down the back of your shirt." Landry made sure to wiggle his butt a little as he climbed the stairs. Muted cursing from behind him told him it was having the desired impact. When he got to his door, Gage was right behind him.

"What was that noxious smell on the landing below?" Gage asked.

"Mr. Lao lives there and he has a thing for incense burners, joss sticks, scented candles…anything stinky. No idea why. It makes me sneeze but I'm developing immunity."

"He should pay you to live here. No one else would put up with that smell."

"My apartment comes with my job, so he kinda does. It could be worse. What if he was addicted to smoked herring, or Cuban cigars? Bleh." Landry headed inside his apartment. "You want to put the snacks in the kitchen? I'll line up some DVDs." He scuttled into the living room, which wasn't too untidy. The old couch was still comfortable and piled with cushions and colorful throws. An antique seaman's chest acted as a coffee table. Landry slipped the disc for *Labyrinth* into his DVD player then turned on a lamp. The windows weren't big and outside the sky had darkened as drizzle turned to rain. *It's a great day to snuggle and watch movies.*

He ventured to the kitchen where Gage had found an assortment of odd bowls to fill with snacks. There were enough goodies to feed a whole tribe, let alone the two of them, but Landry had no objection to that kind of challenge.

"They look yum. What about drinks? I could make hot chocolate, or I have sodas."

"Hot chocolate for me," Gage said. His hip made contact with Landry as they squeezed around each other in the small space. "You've got marshmallows, right?"

"Do bears sit in the woods?" Landry reached for the tin on a high shelf. His top rode up, exposing bare midriff. Behind him, Gage slipped his arm around Landry's waist and pressed a warm hand over his belly. Landry giggled. "I'm ticklish there!"

"Couldn't resist. Warm, naked skin is meant to be touched."

Landry leaned back against Gage's body. "You're warm too." He didn't want Gage to move his hand but it had to happen if he was going to make drinks, or do anything requiring coordination, because he couldn't focus on anything but the sensation of skin on skin.

"Are you purring?" Gage chuckled.

"Maybe?"

"Make the drinks, brat. I'll take the snacks through to the living room." The instant Gage left the kitchen, Landry missed him. He bounced on his toes waiting for the milk to boil because he wanted to get back to touching. The chocolate took a decade to melt in the milk and Landry regretted offering the drink at all — soda would have taken a fraction of the time. In his haste to get to the living room he banged his arm on the doorframe—the same arm that he'd hurt when James Ellery had landed on him.

"Fuckety fuck!" He put the chocolate down on the makeshift coffee table then rubbed at the offending limb.

"Did you hurt yourself?" Gage was on his feet in an instant.

"The English dude landed on me when he fell through the door."

Gage pushed Landry's sleeve up. He was gentle as he manipulated Landry's arm. "You have quite a bruise. It's going to be sore for a while—do you have an ice pack?"

"I have Band-Aids and Tylenol. That's it."

"I'll have to get you a proper first aid kit. You should be better prepared."

"I work in an antique store—it's not that dangerous an environment."

"But you're seeing a cop and I have been known to pick up the odd scrape or two. I think you'd enjoy playing nurse."

"I'm not dressing up for you! I'm kinky but even I have boundaries."

Gage snorted with laughter. "I'm not sure a nurse costume is that much of a boundary, but don't panic, it's not my thing." He sat, pulling Landry onto his lap. "I don't like that he hurt you, even if it was accidental."

"He's coming to the shop tomorrow. I said I'd answer his questions. It was the only way I could think to get rid of him. I wish I'd known you were coming because if I'd waited five more minutes, I wouldn't have offered."

"You don't have to talk to him," Gage said. "He's not law enforcement. You can tell him to take a hike if you want to."

"Then he'll keep coming back and I can't tell him anything useful. Once he knows that, he'll find someone else to harass and besides, he'll have to fit in between customers. With any luck it'll be too busy for me to spare him much time. Let's forget him and enjoy our day—I have so many films you need to watch."

"There's something else we need to talk about first." Gage had put his satchel next to the couch. He groped inside it, pulling out a package that he handed to Landry. "Take a look."

Landry slid a box from its paper wrapping. He had a suspicion he knew what it contained but still gasped when he eased the lid off to reveal a shiny, stainless steel contraption. He lifted it from the box, the metal cold against his fingers. It was smooth, tactile and a little terrifying.

"Have you ever handled a chastity device before?" Gage asked.

Landry shook his head. "I've seen them, of course. At Scorch and on the internet."

"There's no need to be scared."

"That's easy for you to say. It *is* kinda pretty." Steel glinted in the lamplight. "But I can't imagine what it would feel like to wear it. I know it was my choice and I don't want to go back on that, but I'm not sure..."

"I'm not going to force you into anything you don't want to do, Landry. Don't forget, you have your safe word."

"What's the appeal, for you, I mean?" Landry asked.

"A few things," Gage replied. "Power exchange, your trust, me having control over something so fundamental, but most of all, the pleasure I can give you when it comes off."

The metal was warming in Landry's hand. He'd already made his decision. "Okay." He didn't trust himself to say anything else. He handed the device to Gage and was glad that Gage didn't query his decision.

"I want you to strip, from the waist down."

Landry squirmed free of Gage's lap. He toed off his shoes then bent to remove his socks. He made a point of meeting Gage's eyes while he dropped his pants. He kicked them away then hooked his thumbs into the sides of his underwear. Gage gave him a nod and a reassuring smile, which was enough to give Landry the courage to take them off. His face heated under Gage's scrutiny and his cock, somewhat reticent about the situation, remained soft.

"Very pretty." Gage moved to the edge of his seat. "Come a little closer." Landry shuffled forward. "Hands behind your back."

While Gage fitted the chastity device, Landry held his breath. The metal encased his shaft completely but the end had a hole in it. The thick metal ring was a snug fit around the base of his balls but wasn't uncomfortable. It wasn't until Gage connected the two pieces, slipping a small padlock into place, that Landry thought about the implications of being locked up. The device was heavy enough to be noticeable—not that he was likely to forget its presence—but it was the glint of pleasure in Gage's eyes that turned Landry on.

"Oh!" His cock made a valiant attempt to swell. Landry danced around in a little circle. "Oh, that's…wow!"

Gage chuckled. "So you do like it."

"I…no! Yes. I don't know! It's weird."

"You can get dressed if you want to. I'll be much less tempted to torment you if you're wearing pants."

Landry didn't bother with underwear or socks but he yanked on his pants. He didn't know where to put himself. All he could think about was how much he wanted to come and that it was now impossible.

"You won't lose the key, will you?"

"Of course not." Gage slipped the tiny key into his shirt pocket then patted it. "It's quite safe."

Landry was dubious. Something so small could easily get lost and then he'd be trapped. He stuck out his lower lip but took a seat next to Gage on the couch. "You're mean."

"I am. Pass me the Cheetos."

Landry huffed but did as Gage asked before grabbing the remote to start the film. "This is the one with David Bowie in it. I can't believe you haven't seen it." He settled against Gage's side, snuggling close. Gage put his arm around Landry's shoulders, tugging him even closer.

"There's nothing like being inside in the warm when it's wet and miserable outside." Gage sipped his hot chocolate. "Is this a kid's film?"

"It's a Landry film and that's all you need to know," Landry said.

"If it's part of the get-to-know-Landry-better process," Gage said, "I'm in."

"Are we… I mean, are we dating?"

"I believe we are." Gage leaned in for a long, slow kiss.

Landry groaned. "No kissing! Not unless you take the thingy off."

"Does kissing me make you hard?" Gage sounded innocent. Landry wasn't fooled.

"Not at the moment it doesn't and you know it. Watch the film."

Gage's laugh vibrated through Landry's body, and after a while he smiled too.

Chapter Seven

Three movies and a bucket-load of sugar drove Landry to the edge of madness. The credits rolled on *The Maze Runner* and he sighed. Gage's lap was comfy—he'd slipped down Gage's body over the course of the day, ending up with his head cushioned by Gage's perfect thighs—but all he could do was fidget and squirm, hyper-aware of the metal lurking beneath his pants.

"I enjoyed that one best so far," Gage said. "What's next?"

"We could watch the sequel, or maybe take a break and order pizza?"

"Pizza sounds great. You can learn a lot about a man by his choice of pizza toppings. Tell me you don't want pineapple."

Landry made retching noises. "Gross!"

"So what is your pizza of choice?"

"I like veggie best. Onions, roast peppers, asparagus, mushrooms…but if you want meat, chicken or ham is fine with me. I don't like pepperoni and I know that makes me a bad person but it's just yuck, and capers should be banned!"

"How about I order an extra-large pie with veggies one side, garlic chicken the other?"

"Sure, but I can order…"

"I have a place on speed dial. How will we know when the delivery gets here?"

"There's a buzzer by the outer gate. It sounds in here and in Mr. Lao's place. I usually answer in the evening because I'm much quicker than Mr. Lao at getting down the stairs. Uh, Gage…I need to pee."

"Go ahead, you don't need to ask permission. I'm not that much of a control freak."

"But…" Landry pointed to his groin, pouting.

"You can go with it on."

Don't wanna. Landry attempted to convey his reticence with narrowed eyes.

"After we've had pizza, if you're good, I'll take it off."

That meant at least another hour. Landry gave a pained sigh but didn't protest. If he did, he suspected Gage might extend the time he remained locked. "I'm always good." He levered himself up, giving Gage's chest a grope as he did. He followed up with a quick kiss. Gage grabbed his hair then pulled him close for a longer, more sensual kiss that left Landry cursing. "You're killing me! My dick doesn't understand what's going on. He's a pacifist. This whole full metal jacket thing you have going on is messing with his psyche."

"Your dick has a psyche?"

"Of course! He has a mind of his own. I suppose yours is kept fully under control?"

"I am not having a conversation with you about genitalia as sentient beings. Go to the bathroom, Landry."

"Yes, Sir." Landry rolled off the couch, swaying a bit as he stood. "Ooh, sugar rush!" He lurched toward the bathroom, leaving Gage shaking his head in apparent disbelief.

Landry closed the bathroom door then leaned on it. He stretched out his fingers, displaying the small key he had just lifted from Gage's shirt pocket. So much power in such a small thing. He rolled it between his fingers. The temptation to unlock the chastity device was fierce but he had a better plan. He tucked the key away.

Relieving himself wasn't as bad as he had feared. It was easy enough to clean up, which he was careful to do thoroughly. He ran damp hands through his hair and rolled his shoulders, wondering if Gage would be able to stay the night. He made a great pillow and Landry hadn't shared his bed with anyone in a long time. *He probably hogs the comforter.* Landry shrugged. He could deal with that if it meant fun, kinky times with Gage.

As he walked back to the living room, the buzzer sounded, announcing someone at the street gate. Gage appeared, wallet in hand.

"I can go down," Landry offered.

"I've got it." Gage strolled past. "I wouldn't mind a soda to go with the pizza."

Landry made a detour to the fridge but after a few minutes, Gage hadn't returned so Landry went out to the landing and leaned over the bannister. "Gage, you okay down there?"

Gage appeared on the first floor. "It wasn't the pizza delivery. There's a guy down here, claims he's Mr. Lao's nephew. He has a crate of stuff and he says his uncle agreed to sell it on consignment."

"I'm on my way." Landry prayed there was no visible evidence of the metal underneath his pants. He jogged down the stairs to find Gage opening the door. "You shut him outside?" Landry asked.

"I don't know him," Gage said. "He could be anyone."

"Mr. L has a big, extended family. He does take stuff in occasionally but he didn't mention anything to me before he left." Landry peered into the yard. "Oh, hey, Eddie."

"Hi, Landry. Who's the Rottweiler?"

Landry sniggered. "This is Gage. He's a...friend. What have you got for me? Mr. L. didn't say you'd be dropping by."

"No... I doubt he'd remember. He said he'd take this stuff ages ago. A neighbor passed away and Uncle did some valuations for the family, but it's taken a while to get through all the legal stuff sorting out the old lady's estate. Her grandson came by with this lot in the week but I can only get over here on a Sunday."

"No problem," Landry said, eyeing the weighty crate. "I won't be able to put anything on sale until Mr. L gets back because I won't know how to price it, but I can sort and catalogue it so it's ready."

"Sounds good to me," Eddie said. "There's no hurry on this that I'm aware of. I don't have room to keep it at my place." He turned with a wave. "Gotta run."

"Sure, thanks..." Landry scowled at the closing gate. "He could have carted it inside."

"He *did* seem in a bit of a hurry to get out of here." Gage lifted the crate with ease. "Where do you want this?"

Landry tore his gaze away from Gage's flexing biceps. "Over here, please." He directed Gage to a corner of the hall behind the door to the shop. "It won't be in the way there." Gage placed the crate in the corner, nudging it into place with his foot. "I could have moved it, you know."

"I know." Gage's expression displayed no sign of doubt. "Go lock the outside gate. You have all the security sense of a goldfish."

Muttering under his breath, Landry secured the gate. He also locked the yard door when he came inside. "Happy?"

"If you promise to do that every time you come in."

"You sound like Mr. L."

"I think your boss and I will get on just fine." Gage patted Landry's ass. "Let's go."

"Wait, we forgot the pizza guy!" Landry cursed and dragged out his keys.

"You go upstairs," Gage said. "I'll go wait on the street."

"Okay. Call it penance for making me lock up." Landry scampered up the stairs to escape the slap Gage aimed at his behind. He tossed his keys from the safety of the landing. "Missed me!"

"I won't miss a second time, Landry." Gage's voice drifted up the stairwell after him.

* * * *

After a pizza and soda break, Landry settled on the couch with a contented sigh. "I love lazy Sundays."

"Me too." Gage returned from the kitchen where he'd been clearing up.

"You can be my house boy any time." Landry blinked.

"And I can keep you in chastity for a very long time," Gage retorted.

"Oh, no fair! You said you'd let me out." Landry pulled his waistband away from his belly and peered inside his pants. "I've been good."

"Really?" Gage's disbelief was insulting.

"I have!"

"So, how about you give me the key you stole from my pocket earlier?"

Landry gulped and his face burned. "You knew?" He handed it over.

"Uh huh." Gage sat down. He patted his thighs. "Pants off. Over my lap."

Landry debated his options. Use his safe word. Make a run for it. Protest or... He slipped from his seat, then dropped his pants. His dick strained against its prison. He was more turned on than he thought at the prospect of a spanking though he would never admit it, even though getting into position involved a measure of graceless scrambling. His toes touched the floor, but he felt very off balance until Gage placed a steadying hand on the small of his back.

"This is humiliating," Landry mumbled.

"It's punishment. It's not supposed to be fun," Gage said. He rubbed a hand over Landry's bare ass. "Six for the key theft. It should be more but I'm in a generous mood."

Landry huffed then yelped as Gage's palm connected with his backside. The initial sting was followed by a spreading warmth.

"I've changed my mind, this *is* supposed to be fun… For me." Gage landed two more strikes. "You really thought you could get away with pickpocketing a cop?"

"It seemed like a good idea at the time," Landry said. "Ow!"

"Four down, two to go. This *is* entertaining."

"I…" Landry's retort was silenced by the final two spanks. He moaned and at least part of the sound was from pleasure.

"I think you enjoyed that more than you were supposed to," Gage said. He stroked Landry's backside, dipping a finger between his cheeks to nudge his hole.

"Oh!" Landry wanted him to go further. He wriggled in an attempt to find a more comfortable position, spreading his legs a little wider.

"Who's in control here, Landry?"

"Is that a trick question? You?"

"The fact that you made that a question means you deserve more punishment. Perhaps I should leave the cage on overnight."

"No! I mean, please don't, Sir. You're in charge, I promise."

Gage chuckled. "I can see I'm going to have a lot of trouble with you." He helped Landry to his feet before settling him on his lap.

Landry winced as his hot skin made contact with Gage's jeans. "So, what do I have to do to convince you to take this thing off?" He glared at the chastity device.

"There's nothing you can do. It's my decision, but you're in luck because I never go back on my word and I did say earlier that I would take it off." Gage positioned Landry so that he sat with his back to Gage's chest and his legs were spread over Gage's thighs. He reached around Landry's body and spent far too long fiddling with the miniature padlock.

"You're doing this on purpose!" Landry complained.

"Be patient. This is finicky as heck." At last, he was able to remove the device. Landry's cock came to attention in record time. He reached for it, only for Gage to slap his hand away.

"No you don't." Gage wrapped his fingers around Landry's straining erection.

Landry couldn't breathe. He didn't dare do or say anything that might change Gage's mind. His desperation to come overrode all lucid thought. His vision blurred and he sank his teeth into his lower lip in the hope that the small pain would stop him from coming like a horny teenager. He could feel the calluses on Gage's palm, the slight roughness of his skin. He focused on Gage's clean, neatly trimmed fingernails, the lines delineating his knuckles, a scar that ran across the back of one finger. Gage jerked him twice and Landry came in an uncontrollable gush, fire burning through his veins.

"Oh God oh God oh God!" Landry's vision blanked and he slumped back against Gage's body. He shuddered, then jerked as he came a little more. "Am I still alive?" Landry murmured. "I'm not sure. I think I need confirmation."

"Imagine how you'd feel if you'd been in chastity for a week, or a month." Gage stroked Landry's hair.

"I'm not sure the frustration would be worth it."

"What if I told you I want permanent control of your orgasms, caged or not?"

"What do you mean?"

"You only get to come if I say you can. No touching at all, except to keep clean or pee."

Landry tilted his head, needing to see Gage's expression. "You're serious."

"I am."

"But what if I can't help myself? Would I be punished?" Landry didn't think he'd mind another spanking.

"Yes."

"How would you know, though? You can't be with me twenty-four hours a day."

"I'd know."

Gage's calm certainty left Landry in no doubt that it was true and, besides, he couldn't lie without glowing like a ripe tomato. He'd give himself away instantly. "I... How about a trial period?"

"We can do that, but let's make it a rolling trial — the rule continues but we review every week."

"But no cage."

"Not to begin with at least, not unless I'm with you."

"Is chastity your biggest kink?" Landry was curious.

"It's up there. I have a few."

"Are you going to tell me, or is it a state secret?"

"Cheeky brat. You first. We can take it in turns."

"Ooh, 'kay, sounds fun. Wait, what if I put you off? I don't wanna do that."

"Anything that doesn't appeal to both of us, we can discuss, though I'm not averse to testing my limits as well as yours."

"That's new," Landry said. "At the club, I've never had a Dom who's been interested in changing for me."

"Then you haven't been mixing with the right kind of Doms. BDSM has to be a two-way thing. It's about mutual pleasure, not me enjoying myself at your expense—that could be mentally damaging at the very least." Gage pulled a throw from the back of the couch to wrap around Landry.

"I've never thought of it like that," Landry said and a little bit of certainty about Gage's motivations slid into place. "I like rubber...wearing it, I mean. I like the smell, the feel against my skin, how tight it is." He shifted around so that he was face-to-face with Gage.

Gage gave a low growl. "I can't wait to see you in it."

"Really?"

"Really." Gage guided Landry's hand to his groin. "See what you do to me?"

"Oh, wow! That's cool...hey, maybe you should wear a cock cage!"

"Do you want another spanking?"

"Well...maybe not right now. Later?"

"Almost definitely."

"Your turn."

"Bondage. Ropes, chains..."

Landry shivered. "Yes, please!"

"On you, not me. Just to be clear."

"Goody!"

"No objections there then?"

"None." Landry rubbed at his wrists, imagining the marks that Gage might create there.

"That's one more for your list then. What else?"

"This is fun! Plugs are good. Really good." Landry wiggled. There was nothing better than having his ass stuffed nice and full.

"I do like the thought of you, plugged, working all day. You wouldn't be allowed to take it out without permission, of course. Something big enough that you couldn't forget it."

"You're gonna make me hard again."

"Fair's fair." Gage shifted in his seat.

"I'm such a selfish pig." Landry rubbed a hand over the bulge in Gage's pants.

"You're not selfish. If I wanted you to do anything, I would have told you."

"I should have asked anyway…I'm asking now. You want my mouth, my hand…or my ass?"

"What wonderful options to have. Are you prepped?"

"I have a kit in the bathroom. I was saving it for later in case you wanted to stay over, but it wouldn't take long…"

"Not sure I can wait."

"I love that you want me so bad." Landry lowered Gage's zipper and his cock sprang free. "No undies! Perfect." Landry gave Gage's dick loving stroke. "God, I want you in me so bad."

"There's plenty of time for that. There's pleasure in anticipation."

"I'm not known for my patience." Landry fondled Gage's shaft. "It feels like velvet." He shifted back a little. "This isn't going to work. I'm bendy, but even I can't turn myself into a pretzel." Tucking the throw around him, he scrambled to the floor between Gage's knees. "Much better. Now, I can get to you without damaging myself. I went to a physiotherapist once when I was a kid. I got injured playing baseball. I saw this tiny Hawaiian lady. She looked so sweet and innocent, but I swear that woman could have had an alternative career in interrogation for the FBI."

Gage gave him a frustrated glare. "You're doing it on purpose, aren't you? Much as I love hearing about your history, I'd rather your mouth was engaged elsewhere."

Landry batted his lashes and smiled. "I don't know what you mean, Sir." He plunged his mouth over Gage's erection.

"Fuck!" Gage grabbed a handful of Landry's hair, holding him in place, giving him just enough latitude to move up and down. Landry sucked hard. He licked around the base of Gage's crown, probing with his tongue, seeking all the most sensitive spots. He knew he was in the right place when Gage's grip on his hair tightened. Humming happily, Landry put all his energy into giving Gage as much pleasure as he knew how. He pulled off to nuzzle Gage's balls, taking their warm weight on his tongue. When he sucked each furry orb into his mouth in turn, Gage jerked and swore.

"You're fucking killing me, Landry."

"Wouldn't want that." Landry sucked harder, sensing Gage was close to the edge. He took him as deep as he could, jaw stretched and aching. When the tip of Gage's cock hit the back of Landry's throat, he swallowed. Gage came with a yell, tugging hard on Landry's hair. Landry savored the taste of Gage's cum on his tongue. He lapped at Gage's dick, licking it clean, before resting back on his heels. Gage let go of Landry's hair with a shuddering breath.

"Holy fuck, you're good at that."

Landry preened. "You taste good." He scrambled back onto Gage's lap. "Do I get more cuddles now?"

"You certainly do."

Chapter Eight

Gage scowled into the darkness, drumming his fingers on the steering wheel. He'd never been so frustrated in his life. It was as if some higher power was determined to keep him away from Landry's exceptionally cute rear. Exchanging the prospect of Landry's warm bed for a long, cold night watching the back entrance of an anonymous warehouse was not his idea of fun. After the call had come in with the tip-off he'd barely had time to get to his assigned spot, let alone stop for coffee, and that had not improved his mood at all. He dialed Sancha.

"I hate my life."

"On a promise, were you?" Sancha knew him far too well. "Did you leave him tied to the bed?"

"That would not be responsible now, would it?" An image of Landry, naked, tied down, begging, flashed into Gage's mind. "Fuck."

"Not gonna get the chance, are you!" Sancha cackled.

"We've been here for four hours. My ass is numb and the only life I've seen has been a couple of mutant-sized rats and some hobo pushing a shopping cart full of beer cans. I was half tempted to ask him if he had any full ones."

"No action here either, but I do have a flask of coffee and a packet of sandwiches."

"What filling?"

"Peanut butter and jelly."

Gage sighed. "This is a fucking waste of time. Where did the tip come from?"

"That information is above our pay grade. One of the lieutenant's oh-so-reliable sources, I'd guess. A shipment of antiques being moved tonight, possibly from the Tokyo raid."

Gage caught movement out of the corner of his eye. He slumped as far down in his seat as he could manage while still being able to see the wing mirror. "Gray van, coming down the street behind me. No lights. This could be it. Stand by." He disconnected the phone and switched to his radio. "Stay in position. We need to wait until they start unloading." He updated the stakeout team then watched in the mirror as the van pulled up next to a roller door. No one got out of the vehicle but the door began to open, making little sound, suggesting that it had been recently oiled. Gage held his breath. He couldn't understand why no one was getting out of the van. Traces of exhaust told him its engine was still running. Without warning, it swung into the center of the street then reversed toward the opening door.

"Fuck, the van is going into the building." He spat the words into the radio. "I'm going to try to get in before the door closes."

"Don't be so fucking stupid," Sancha yelled. "Wait for backup."

"Give me five minutes, then raid from the other entrance."

Once the windshield of the van edged from view, Gage slipped from his car and, keeping to a crouch, he scuttled across the road. He pressed against the wall of the warehouse, gun in hand. When the shutter lowered to a foot above the ground, he dropped and rolled, making it inside seconds before the shutter closed. The slight clang as metal hit concrete disguised the sound of him sliding beneath the front of the van, where he froze in place. The clunk of van doors, followed by heavy footsteps, told him that at least two occupants had exited the vehicle. They circled to the back doors and yanked them open.

"Let's make this quick." The gruff statement was met with a grunt.

Gage shifted, trying to get closer. He didn't want to reveal himself until his colleagues had gained access to the other end of the building. His knee hit something hard and metal.

"What the fuck was that?"

"It came from under the van." Dirty boots appeared far too close to Gage's face. He rolled the other way, only to be dragged from under the van. He kicked hard but was forced to his knees. He raised his gun, but a wrench connected with his wrist, compelling him to drop it as pain shot up his arm. The weapon skittered across the floor and a fist connected with his jaw.

"Fucking cop."

"He's seen our faces. Kill him. Then let's get out of here."

In an attempt to buy some time, Gage spat on the nearest boot. Saliva mixed with blood spattered the leather.

"Filthy pig."

Gage braced for another blow but shouts of "Stop, Seattle PD!" echoed through the space. He threw himself to one side, reaching for his gun. He grabbed it and got one shot off into the van's tire before a line of searing fire crossed his shoulder. There were more shots and shouting. Gage kept his head down, pressing his body flat to the floor. Only when the shooting stopped did he dare roll over, to find Sancha looming over him, her face like thunder.

"Could you be any more of a fucking idiot?"

Gage doubted there was a correct answer to that question, so he settled for what he hoped was a disarming grin.

"I should shoot you myself."

"I think they beat you to it." Gage pressed a hand over his shoulder. His fingers came back bloody. Sancha knocked his hand away.

"It's a flesh wound, you lucky son of a bitch. I swear you're going to give me a coronary one of these days."

"You love me really." Gage staggered to his feet. The warehouse was swarming with cops who were poking into the van, investigating the stacks of boxes and dealing with the two bodies stretched out on the ground.

"Why did you shoot the tire instead of one of them?" Sancha had her hands on her hips.

"Didn't want them to get away." Gage shrugged, instantly regretting the action. "Fuck, that hurts."

"You're doing the fucking paperwork on this one because it's gonna take a week *and* you're buying me lunch tomorrow." Sancha kept muttering under her breath as she guided Gage to the warehouse's other entrance, where paramedics had arrived. "This idiot needs a Band-Aid." She pushed him toward a bewildered medic. "Not that he deserves one. Don't be nice to him. Make it hurt."

"It's because she cares," Gage reassured the young woman, and it was true. He knew Sancha's reaction was because she worried about him and she was right. He probably should have waited for backup, but four hours sitting around had made him stir crazy. He caught Sancha's eye. "Was it worth it? Have they found anything?"

"I'll go find out. Don't move."

"Not going anywhere." Gage submitted to the ministrations of the paramedic without complaint. "Tell me I don't need stitches."

"You don't. You've lost a strip of skin. It's messy and it's going to hurt like hell for a while but I'll clean it up—there could be fragments of your shirt in the wound. Then keep it covered with sterile dressings for a few days. You'll have a narrow scar, not much more than a line."

By the time the medic was done, Sancha had returned clutching a piece of paper. "They found paintings and some silverware. No jewelry. The van crew were collecting, not delivering, so the stuff could have been there a while. There was also this note in one of the dead guys' pockets." She held it out.

Gage unfolded the single, lined sheet, which looked like it had been torn from a cheap notebook. "*Find the key*. Did they have a key?"

"Nope. Well, just the one for the van, which is a rental by the way. No identification of any kind."

"Professionals then."

"Not very good ones, considering they're both full of holes. They had no intention of giving themselves up, which suggests the consequences of failure would have been severe. Lovely bunch."

"Doesn't help us though, does it? It would have been helpful to have live bodies to question."

"Go home, Gage. Tomorrow is soon enough to start wading through the paperwork mountain." Sancha yawned. "Bring me coffee and donuts or your life won't be worth living."

"No promises. Thanks for having my back, S."

"I don't have time to break in a new partner. It's taken me long enough to beat you into shape." She marched off and didn't look back.

* * * *

Landry made a star shape in his bed, wishing he didn't have the space. The evening had gone so well and he'd been beyond happy when Gage had said he could stay the night, but then Gage's stupid phone had made beepy noises and after a muttered conversation with whoever was on the other end, he'd left. Not before giving Landry the best kiss ever, admittedly, but it wasn't the same as a night of wild, energetic sexy times. He hadn't slept well, and by the time his alarm sounded, Landry had the mother of all headaches. It wasn't the best way to start his first day in charge of Treasure Trove.

He scraped himself out of bed, took a lukewarm shower because the water was playing up, then yanked on jeans and a plain navy long sleeved T-shirt. He had plenty of tops with snarky slogans but Mr. Lao didn't like him wearing them when he was working. Landry thought that was a shame, because there were quite a few customers that could do with a humor injection.

His stomach rebelled at the thought of food so he saved the few precious minutes that would normally have been dedicated to a bowl of Lucky Charms and used them to make an extra-large coffee in his lidded cup. He breathed in the aroma with a sigh. The first cup was always the best.

After swallowing two painkillers and grabbing his keys, he stumbled downstairs, leaving his coffee on a step while he went through the laborious process of unlocking the back door, yard gate and security shutters. He made sure to relock the gate and door on the way back inside, partly because Gage might come by and check but also because Landry didn't want any more surprise visitors. He let himself into the store, turned the 'closed' sign to 'open' and unbolted the front door. *Finally. Fort Knox is now open for business.*

Next came the ritual of the light switches. Rather than glaring overhead lights, there was a range of lamps dotted around the place. Most were rewired antiques and part of the stock but until they sold, they earned their space by illuminating the cavernous store. Once that was done, Landry thought he deserved a coffee break. On a Monday morning he was unlikely to see a customer before ten, if then. He settled in his chair behind the cash desk and closed his eyes. A few sips of coffee helped his mood but not the nagging ache that formed a tight band around his head. The painkillers either hadn't kicked in or given him up as a lost cause. He knuckled his temples, tilting his head from side to side. His neck gave an ominous crack. Rolling his shoulders produced more creaking sounds. "Anyone would think I was fifty-five, not twenty-five. I need a massage in the worst way. Ought to stop talking to myself too — it's not a good look."

After fifteen minutes of quiet contemplation, Landry fetched his special duster from the supply closet and got to cleaning. Old furniture attracted dust like a magnet but he did find the polishing part of his job therapeutic. Mr. Lao used a brand of beeswax-based polish that came in a squat jar and smelled of almonds. It only took a dab and a bit of elbow grease to bring up a glow. When the bell over the door rang just before eleven, Landry was almost done. He shoved his cleaning materials into a convenient rose-patterned chamber pot then wandered back to the cash desk, keeping an eye out for customers. He didn't see anyone and wondered if he had imagined the bell but then a creaky floorboard betrayed whoever was hiding in the aisles.

"Can I help you?" Landry didn't want to have to tackle a thief so early in the day.

"I can think of many ways I could respond to that offer." The English accent was a giveaway.

Landry suppressed a groan. "Do you have some kind of qualification in skulking?"

"Of course, it's in the job description."

"Can this shitty day get any worse?" Landry muttered. "Hello, Mr. Ellery."

"Call me James." James Ellery held out a tall take-out cup.

"Is that a bribe?" Despite himself, Landry licked his lips.

"Call it a peace offering. I had to guess what you might like. I got you an extra hot, extra foam, double shot, vanilla latte."

"Oh my God, gimme!" Landry made a grab for the cup, his self-respect in tatters. "This doesn't mean I like you."

"Of course not." James' eyes twinkled.

They actually twinkled. He looks like a fucking movie star. Landry took in the designer jeans, gleaming white shirt and pale blue Burberry sweater, which had to be cashmere. A trace of stubble stopped James from being too pretty. "I'm busy. I can give you ten minutes."

"Yes, I can see you're overrun with customers." James glanced around the empty store.

Landry huffed. "No people doesn't mean no work. I'm sure your job is the most important thing in the world, but here, I'm in charge. If I say I'm busy, I'm busy."

"Maybe vanilla wasn't your flavor after all." James grinned.

"If only you knew." Landry scowled. He wondered if James had a Dommy streak. *Pure sadist, I'd guess.*

"So is the guy you were with yesterday your boyfriend?"

"I don't think that's any of your business."

"It is if I want to ask you to dinner."

Landry gaped. "You've got a nerve! One coffee does not buy you a date." *You do have a cute accent, though.*

"That wasn't a no."

"No!" Landry retreated behind the cash desk.

James was still smiling. "I don't give up easily."

"I'm with Gage. I don't cheat." Landry sipped his coffee. "Oh God, that's good." *Unless drinking another man's coffee counts as cheating.*

James shrugged. "We'll see."

"Did you come in here to irritate me or do you have questions? I'm beginning to wonder."

"What do you know about international jewel theft?"

"Nothing. Well, I know it happens," Landry said. "Sometimes we get pictures from the cops asking us to look out for certain pieces, but Mr. Lao is careful about provenance."

"Where does he get his inventory?"

"Auctions, private sales, other dealers. He sometimes takes items on consignment." Landry gulped more coffee. "But we don't sell that much jewelry. Mr. Lao specializes in furniture... As you can see." Landry waved at the teetering piles of stock.

"Clearly. There's more wood in here than in the New Forest."

"Huh?"

"It's in Hampshire."

"The only British forest I've heard of is Sherwood."

"Which isn't as big as the movies would have you believe. Who's your favorite Robin Hood? Please don't say the Disney fox."

Landry huffed. "Michael Praed. Why am I even discussing this with you?"

"Nice choice and because I'd like us to be friends."

"Please get to the point. One coffee only buys you so much of my patience."

"Jewelry specialists are the least likely channel for international thieves to distribute stolen items because the honest ones will be alert to suspect pieces and the dishonest ones are on the authorities' radars. Much easier to slip something to an unsuspecting mark."

"Mr. Lao isn't an idiot," Landry said. "He's careful. You're welcome to take a look at what we have on display, though the police have already been here so you'd be wasting your time."

"I've already looked."

"Of course you have." Landry scowled. "I don't get it. Why all the interest? Like I said, we've had pictures come through from the cops before, stolen goods from break-ins usually. Wouldn't professionals sell direct to unscrupulous collectors?"

"Not in this case."

"This case?"

"I'm telling you too much... A few weeks ago, a collection of antique jewelry, paintings and porcelain belonging to the family of a 1940s film star was stolen from an exhibition in Tokyo. The company I work for insured the collection, which was worth several million dollars. One piece, a sculpture, showed up in London two weeks ago. A painting was found in Berne the week before. Intelligence is that the rest of the collection has been smuggled into the US and disappeared."

"Intelligence or rumor?"

"A bit of both. We think the thieves are desperate to get rid of the goods. They'll either surface or be gone forever — to the unscrupulous private buyers you mentioned."

"And that wouldn't be good for your commission."

"Well I do like to treat my dates in style."

"Lucky them."

"Could be lucky you...that's if you're feeling adventurous."

"You don't know when to give up, do you?"

James smiled, though it didn't reach his eyes. "Never."

Landry held back a shiver. There was no doubt that James was gorgeous but there was something about him that made Landry nervous. He suspected that beneath the suave exterior lurked something far more dangerous. That did have some appeal. Landry wasn't averse to an occasional walk on the wild side.

"I think we're done here. I have your card if I see or hear anything suspicious." The bell over the shop door jangled and it opened to emit a gaggle of pink-haired ladies. "I need to get back to work."

"Timing is everything." James grabbed Landry's hand then held it to his lips, kissing it softly. "Until we meet again. Feel free to use my number any time."

"I…" Landry pulled his hand away, though not as quickly as he should have. He rubbed at the back of it, trying to come up with a suitably scathing retort, but he wasn't thinking straight and when he looked up, James Ellery had gone.

Chapter Nine

By the end of the day, Landry was exhausted and the nagging headache he'd started out with remained. He heaved the security shutter into place, cursing the persistent shower that had started the instant he walked outside. He fumbled with the padlock, grazing his knuckles on the shutter as it finally clicked shut.

"Ow." He sucked the back of his hand, gagging at the metallic taste of blood. Feeling a bit nauseous, he staggered around the corner to the back gate, which was ajar. "Could have sworn I closed it." He shrugged. "Wind must have blown it open." He cursed his keys and the lock, getting wetter the longer he took, but managed to secure the gate. Turning, he headed across the yard, but froze when he spotted a figure sheltering in the doorway.

"Don't panic. It's me."

"Gage!" Landry's pounding heart slowed. "You scared me."

"Good, that was the idea. I could have been anyone and you could have trapped yourself in here with a mugger. I don't suppose you locked this door behind you when you came out here either, did you?" He nudged it with his ass, pushing it open. "Thought not."

Landry scuffed the toe of his sneaker against the concrete. "Sorry. I wanted to be quick because of the rain."

"Get inside. You have water dripping off your nose."

Landry sighed. He didn't want Gage to be angry with him. He knew he should have been more careful about security but he was tired, hungry and just wanted to collapse on the couch. He trudged inside where Gage took his keys then locked the door before shoving him against the wall for a long, slow kiss.

"I'm not angry, I want you to be safe."

"Sorry." Landry fought to hold back tears. His lower lip wobbled.

"Hey…it's okay." Gage tilted Landry's chin and his expression was so concerned Landry sobbed.

"I didn't mean to…but I've been on my own all day and it was busy and I didn't get a lunch break and forgot to order food and I only got two coffees and one was delivered by that British guy." His voice trailed off into a wail. "I'm so tired and this is only the first day Mr. Lao is away. I never realized how much he did around the place. There's so much to remember." He sniffled.

"I brought Chinese food." Gage held up an arm to display the bag dangling from his wrist.

"Can I marry you and have your babies?" Landry thrust his head into the bag, breathing in the savory aromas.

Gage shook his head. "I'm not eating in the hall. Let's go upstairs, shall we?"

The prospect of food gave Landry renewed energy and he bounced up the stairs, scrubbing the tears from his face as he went. "Are you gonna get called out again tonight or can you stay? I'm not sure I can stand the disappointment two nights in a row—a boy could develop a complex." Landry retrieved plates and forks from the kitchen. "I'm hopeless with chopsticks and way too hungry to deal with one grain of rice at a time. What did you get?"

Gage unloaded the cartons onto Landry's small dining table. "A mixture because I didn't know what you'd prefer. There's sesame chicken, moo shu pork, shrimp with cashews, crispy beef in garlic, mixed vegetables and fried rice."

"Okay, that's my dinner. What are you having?" Landry opened all the cartons then started loading his plate with food. "This smells so good."

"There's plenty for both of us, piglet, and yes, I can stay. There's always a chance I'll get a call but that's the job."

"Can you tell me what happened last night, or is it confidential?" Instead of sitting at the table, Landry lugged his plate over to the couch. Comfort food demanded comfortable seating. Gage came to sit next to him.

"We got a tip-off about stolen goods being moved. I spent four cold, boring hours watching a warehouse in a not-so-great part of town."

"And that was it?" Landry spoke around a mouthful of rice.

"We got the bad guys. Can't really say anything else."

"Wow! So it was worth it in the end?"

"Sure. It paid off. More often than not, nothing happens."

Landry rested his head on Gage's shoulder. "I'm glad you're here."

"Yeah, me too…but do you think you could switch sides?" Gage's face was pale and drawn.

"Oh my God, you're hurt! What the hell…why didn't you tell me?" Landry dumped his half-empty plate on the coffee table. "Show me. Right now, buster."

Gage sighed. "Can't we finish eating first?"

"No!"

Gage had hardly put his plate down before Landry attacked his shirt buttons. "You just want to get my clothes off. Let me." Gage eased out of his shirt, revealing a large dressing covering most of his shoulder and biceps.

Landry petted Gage's chest. "What's under the dressing?"

"Bullet wound."

"What the fuck!" Landry yelled. "Why didn't you call me or, at the very least, tell me right away when you got here tonight?"

"It's just a scrape. Bullet dug a groove in my shoulder, that's all. The bad guy missed me. Can I put my shirt back on now?"

"No." Landry pouted. "Let's call it payback for you not letting on were hurt. Besides, I like your chest." He planted a kiss on one hard pec.

"I thought you were starving?" Gage reached for his plate.

"I am." Landry grabbed his too but kept glancing at Gage's arm while he ate. "Does it hurt?"

"Yes."

"Have you had any pain medication?"

"I don't like taking drugs."

"You're an idiot."

"Have you been comparing notes with my partner, Sancha?"

"She sounds like the kind of woman I'd get on with. You want seconds?"

Gage shook his head so Landry filled his own plate again. "Thank you for bringing all this. I couldn't face going out for food tonight so I was contemplating an omelet. You're still an idiot. I can't believe you got yourself shot!"

"I didn't…never mind." Gage closed his eyes. "It was a long night and an even longer day."

"We make quite a pair," Landry said. "How much sleep have you had?"

"Uh, three hours, I think."

"You wanna go to bed?" Landry scooped up both plates and took them to the kitchen. Gage followed.

"Bed sounds really good. I'm too tired to think carnal thoughts, though."

"Me too. You can hold me, though, right? I really need a cuddle."

"That I can do."

Landry grabbed Gage's hand then led him to the bedroom, a cozy riot of color, soft pillows and throws. "I'm gonna go clean my teeth and wash up a bit. I have a spare toothbrush somewhere. I'll dig it out for you."

"Thanks, I'd appreciate that. Much as I love Chinese food, I don't want to be tasting it for the rest of the night."

Landry scurried to the bathroom, took the quickest shower in the history of the world then brushed his teeth. He hoped Gage would be able to manage a few kisses before he lost consciousness. Landry offered a wry smile to his reflection in the mirror over the sink. *Life sure gets in the way sometimes.* He found a spare toothbrush and a package of disposable razors in case Gage wanted to shave. He kind of hoped not. Gage's stubble against his skin was hot as hell. Naked, he ambled back to the bedroom where he found Gage, stretched out on the bed.

"Are you still awake?"

"I am now." Gage leered.

"There didn't seem much point in getting dressed again after my shower and I always sleep naked," Landry said. "Unless you prefer I put on some jammies?"

"No!"

Landry grinned at the urgency in Gage's voice.

"What's with the audience?" Gage gestured at the shelf holding Landry's lucky cat collection.

"I've been collecting them since I was a kid. They're all rejects. I like the bright colors and they're supposed to be lucky."

"It could be worse, I suppose," Gage said. "You could collect plushies."

"There's nothing wrong with plushies!" Landry felt the need to defend soft toys. "I left some supplies in the bathroom for you."

"Cool. I had a shower before I came over but didn't think to bring an overnight bag. I didn't want to assume, I suppose."

"When it comes to having you in my bed, you can be as presumptuous as you like."

Grinning, Gage swung his legs off the bed. He stood, then stalked toward Landry. Landry sank his teeth into his bottom lip, lowering his eyes.

"I don't believe you suddenly got shy, sweetheart." Gage wrapped Landry in his arms. He stroked Landry's back, letting his hand come to rest on the swell of Landry's ass. "This will be mine. Is mine."

Landry snuggled against Gage's bare chest. "Soon, I hope."

"Warm the bed up for me." Gage gave Landry's ass a soft slap. "I won't be long." He left for the bathroom and Landry immediately felt cold. He scrambled beneath the covers, half hard despite his fatigue. The prospect of a night tucked against Gage's strong body gave him the shivers. Maybe in the morning there would be time for more.

* * * *

Despite Landry's hopes for early morning fun times, the alarm on Gage's phone went off at stupid o'clock. Landry only awoke fully when Gage tried to extricate himself from under Landry's body. Sometime in the night, he had decided to use Gage as a mattress.

"Go back to sleep, it's early. Sorry."

"Do you always start work in the middle of the night?" Landry mumbled.

"I need to go home for fresh clothes before I go into the station. It'll take a while and Sancha does not appreciate tardiness."

"Sounds like a scary lady." Landry yawned.

"Like you wouldn't believe."

"I can get up, make you coffee."

"No, I'll grab something at the drive-through. Sleep. You need it."

"Will you be back tonight?" Landry tried not to sound too needy.

"I hope so, but I can't promise. Where's my shirt?"

"You left it on the couch. Bring an overnight bag this time."

Gage bent over Landry then gave him a gentle kiss. "Have a good day."

"Wait, you'll need keys to get out." Landry groped in the drawer of his nightstand. "Take the spare set then you can let yourself in any time."

Gage took them, a strange expression on his face. "It's the first time anyone's ever given me keys to their place."

Landry gave him a lazy smile. He pushed the covers down to his knees, revealing his rigid erection. He took a firm hold of his warm shaft. "If you've got them, you won't forget me."

"I've never met a sub more in need of discipline than you. You've already forgotten the rule about not touching yourself without my permission."

"I *can* be forgetful," Landry said, tugging on his dick.

"And I can be cruel. I'll be sure to pack a flogger in my overnight bag if I get back tonight. You're getting off light… If I didn't have to go…"

Landry ran his tongue across his lower lip. "Have a good day. No getting shot again."

"I'll try not to. Dammit…" Gage grabbed Landry, rolling him onto his front. He gave his backside six hard spanks. "Something to remember me by while you're working today and *not* touching yourself. Be good."

Landry moaned into his pillow. Heat spread across his skin. He stuck his ass in the air, hoping for more, but the click of his apartment door told him he'd have to wait.

* * * *

The morning in the shop passed quickly but Landry did get time to call Basim at the diner and get some lunch sent down so he could eat while he closed for an hour. By early afternoon, the customers had cleared and he had a few moments to relax. He decided to sort through the crate Mr. Lao's nephew had left two nights before. He dragged it into the shop so that it sat behind the cash desk and wasn't cluttering up the aisles. Once he'd ripped off the packing tape that held the box closed, he could see that everything inside had been individually wrapped in newspaper. It wasn't much protection and he hoped that nothing had been damaged in transit.

It was kind of fun discovering the contents of each package. The first thing he unwrapped proved to be a gorgeous ginger jar complete with lid. Landry guessed it dated from around 1930 and was a lovely example, decorated with butterflies and scrolling flowers and foliage. It measured about seven inches tall, and the same in diameter. He couldn't spot any dings, damage or restoration so it was in great condition and he could see why Mr. Lao would have picked it out. He put it carefully on the counter and unwrapped the next object. He laughed at the pair of comical hardwood figures depicting two water buffalo, which were lying down and each had a boy climbing on its back. The expressions of the buffalo were brilliantly captured. He guessed that the inset eyes were glass and the teeth appeared to be made from bone. Landry couldn't guess their age because he didn't think Mr. Lao had had anything similar in the shop recently. He went on to unwrap an eighteenth-century painting of a pair of quails, a large soapstone sculpture of two parakeets and an ornate clock, topped with a gilt Chinese dragon. There were also two jade necklaces, several vases in varying condition and a silver bonbon dish. His favorite item was a nineteenth-century lacquered sewing box decorated with Chinese court scenes, the wood a beautiful mellow color.

Landry thought everything would sell really quickly once Mr. Lao was able to price it. In the meantime, Landry would have to move it onto storage shelves in the small back room where they kept stock awaiting display. He sifted through loose newspaper in the bottom of the box and found he had missed one item. "Oh, oh wow!" It proved to be what he thought was a maneki neko, a lucky cat made from porcelain, but one of its ears was chipped. It had a really cute expression. It was very different from the small collection of lucky cats in Landry's bedroom, and he remembered Mr. Lao giving him a lesson in the differences between Japanese and Chinese versions. This one was Japanese and he wondered why it had been in the box when everything else was exclusively Chinese. Because it was damaged, he decided to take it up to his apartment later. Perhaps it would bring him some luck — though he'd have to return it if Mr. Lao thought it had value.

It took Landry a while to move everything to the storage closet and clear up the box and paper, by which time more customers had come into the store and he had to get back to work. He was helping a regular decide between oak or pine for a blanket box when he spotted the car parked on the other side of the street. It was raining again and getting dark, so he couldn't identify the model, but it was a black sedan with tinted windows. What had caught his eye, he realized as it happened again, was the orange glow of a lit cigarette as a smoker in the car inhaled. It seemed strange that someone would be smoking without cracking the window a bit. It was also unusual for an occupied car to be parked there at all.

"Have you got someone waiting for you, Mr. Lowenstein?" Landry asked his customer.

"No, son. I'll be sending my daughter to pick up the box. I like to walk and you know my place isn't far from here. Why do you ask?"

"Just a car idling out there. Must be for someone else. Ignore me."

"I've decided on the oak. You want to ring me up?"

"Good choice. I prefer that one too — it's such a warm, golden shade." Landry walked Mr. Lowenstein to the register. "I can give you a ten percent discount as you're such a great customer."

"You're a good boy. You always look after me." He handed over his credit card. Landry hand wrote a receipt and recorded the sale in the ledger. "I'll put a 'sold' label on it right away."

"Rebecca will be in this weekend."

"No problem." Mr. Lowenstein slipped Landry a ten-dollar bill.

"You know, you don't have to do that."

"It's my pleasure, young man. You provide good service and that's a rarity in this day and age."

"Well, thank you, I appreciate it." Landry escorted Mr. Lowenstein to the door, using it as an opportunity to check if the car was still parked opposite the shop. He opened the door, setting the bells jangling. "Have a good evening." The car *was* still there. There was an hour to go before Landry could close up and he was now alone in the store. He peered between the goods in the window to see if he could spot who might be in the car, but it was impossible and the light was fading fast. "I'm probably being paranoid," he muttered, but when he got back to the cash desk he picked up his phone and dialed Gage's number.

"Roskam." Gage sounded impatient.

"Oh, hi, Gage... It's Landry. I'm sorry if I'm disturbing you. I shouldn't have called."

"It's fine," Gage said, his tone softening. "It's nice to hear your voice. How's your day been?"

"Okay. Busy."

"What's wrong, Landry? You sound worried. Has that English idiot come back again?"

"No, I haven't seen him, but there is something... Probably nothing. Now that I've called you, I feel stupid."

"Tell me. Right now, Landry."

"There's a car parked outside, opposite the shop. It's been there a while and it has its engine running. I'm pretty sure there's someone inside it because I think I saw the glow of a cigarette. I haven't been able to watch it the whole time because I've been dealing with customers and I don't know how long it had been there before I spotted it, but it seems a bit odd. People who park on the street tend to get out and go into the local businesses. They don't just sit there, not for so long anyway."

"Can you see the plates?"

"Not from here. I could if I go around to the side gate, but the shop's still open and I can't leave it."

"Give me five minutes, I'll get some uniforms to drive by. They can get the plates and make it obvious that they're checking the vehicle out."

"Really? I don't want to get you into trouble for doing something you shouldn't."

"You're reporting a suspicious vehicle and that's perfectly legitimate. There will be a patrol in the area and it won't take them a moment to have a look. I need to get off the phone to sort this out, okay?"

"Sure. Thanks, Gage. I hope I'm not wasting anyone's time."

"You're not. And I will be by later."

Landry hovered behind the cash desk, not sure whether to stay where he was or take another look out of the window. He edged down the center aisle but before he got to the door, a Seattle PD patrol car cruised past. It stopped and two officers got out. They started across the street, hands on their holsters, but before they reached the strange car it peeled away, narrowly missing them. Landry gasped and flung open the door.

"Are you guys okay?"

One of the cops was talking into his radio while the other came toward Landry. "Are you the one that called this in?"

Landry nodded. "I wasn't sure…"

"Seems like you were right to be concerned. We'll run the plates and report back to Detective Roskam. I suggest you go inside, sir. Leave this to us."

Both cops got into their vehicle then did a U-turn and sped off in the same direction as the mysterious car. Landry shivered and flicked the catch on the shop door. If any more customers came, he would hear them.

Chapter Ten

"Thank you for texting that you were on your way. I'm still a bit spooked. Hearing somebody coming into the apartment would have given me a heart attack." Landry sat cross-legged on his bed watching Gage unpack his overnight bag.

"I'm sorry I'm so late. When we ran the plates on the car, it came back as stolen, so I got hold of the CCTV footage for part of the route. We got a nice clear image of the driver and passenger in the car when they pulled up at a stop light. It didn't take long to get a match on their pictures."

"So who were they?" Landry asked the question, even though he wasn't sure he wanted to know the answer.

"Bōryokudan. More commonly known as Yakuza."

"That's the Japanese mafia, isn't it?"

"Organized crime syndicate, yes. The two men we identified are low=level members of a group known to be operating in Seattle. Hired muscle."

"So was it just a coincidence that they were parked on the street here? Having a coffee break maybe?" Landry asked hopefully.

"I doubt it, but we're unlikely to find them I'm afraid. False plates on the car…they'll be long gone. There was too much traffic to warrant a high-speed chase. The question is, why were they watching you?"

"I have no idea. They could have been watching another business, couldn't they? Do you think it's something to do with the case you're working on?"

"Well, I don't believe in coincidences but it's too late to do anything more about it today." Gage stretched, yawned. "I have to be up early and so do you."

"I don't know if I'm going to be able to sleep."

Gage took off his pullover, mussing his hair as he did. "Oh, I can think of a few ways to wear you out. And besides, I owe you a punishment from this morning. The kind of teasing you engaged in demands the stiffest of penalties. By rights, I should lock you in chastity for at least a week."

Landry gaped. "You wouldn't." *Though stiff penalties sound kinda good.*

"Of course I would, but you're in luck because I didn't bring the cage with me."

Landry let out the breath he'd been holding. "That's…fortunate."

"Bad planning on my part, but I brought something else instead." Gage dumped a tangle of leather and chains on the bed. "Take your clothes off, Landry."

Swallowing, Landry tried to work out what Gage was planning. His cock, already half hard just from watching Gage remove his sweater, stiffened further. He clambered off the bed then undressed, folding his clothes as he went. His skimpy Batman underwear was doing little to contain his erection.

"Stop." Gage, still wearing his T-shirt and jeans, stalked around the bed. He patted Landry's ass. "Are you ready for me?"

"Yes, Sir." Hanging around waiting for Gage to turn up had given Landry plenty of time to prepare.

"Good boy." Gage slid a hand under the silky fabric of Landry's briefs to squeeze his backside. "You weren't good this morning, were you? Deliberately flouting my rules has to be addressed. After I'd left, did you come?"

Landry nodded, his face heating. "I couldn't help it."

"Sir."

"I couldn't help it, Sir. I was frustrated because you had to leave."

"So you're saying it was my fault that you touched yourself, blatantly, in front of me?"

"Yes?" Landry attempted to look innocent.

"Spare me, you little brat. You knew exactly what you were doing and you were enjoying it."

Gage picked up the leather and chain spaghetti from the bed. With a bit of deft untangling, he freed a leather belt with two wide wrist cuffs attached to it by short lengths of chain. He fastened the belt around Landry's waist, cinching it tight, then he buckled one of Landry's wrists into each of the cuffs. Landry found that he could only move his hands a couple of inches in either direction. There was no way he could reach anything interesting. Nor could he undo the cuffs or the belt.

"Very nice. Now, I want you to lie on the bed and spread your legs apart."

It was awkward, but Landry found that by using his elbows and wiggling his butt, he could get into position. Gage adjusted the pillows so that Landry's head was supported. "Have you ever been edged?"

"No." Landry gulped.

"Then I shall enjoy showing you how it works," Gage said. He stripped to his underwear—navy-blue boxer briefs that Landry really, *really* wanted to investigate.

"I know what it is," Landry said, trying not to sound desperate.

"I'm sure you do."

"Then shouldn't we discuss it?"

"This relationship is not a democracy. Spread your legs a little wider."

"It isn't?"

"I'd say it's more of a benevolent dictatorship."

"Not so benevolent from where I'm lying," Landry muttered. His balls ached and his dick seemed to be in accord with the whole dictatorship thing.

"You have a safe word, Landry. Nice choice of underwear, by the way."

"Stop smiling. They're comfortable and fun. There's nothing wrong with that and, besides, Batman is a stud."

"The positioning of the bat. That's...interesting." Gage yanked Landry's underwear down so that the elastic waistband wedged beneath his balls.

"Oh!"

"Where's your lube?"

"Nightstand drawer."

Gage pulled the drawer open. He produced the dispenser of lube and then Landry's favorite dildo. "Interesting."

Landry's face heated. "A boy has to be able to entertain himself."

"Not anymore, you don't." Gage slathered the toy with lube. "Pull your knees up." When Landry's knees were somewhere near his ears, Gage pressed the end of the sizeable rubber dildo to Landry's hole. "Deep breaths." He applied steady pressure and Landry's eager body swallowed the toy with little more than a slight burn. Gage pushed it in and out a few times, making Landry squeal. "Okay, legs down. That'll give you something to think about other than your dick."

Landry clenched his inner muscles, working the toy hard. "Feels so good... Need to come."

"Not gonna happen any time soon." Gage pumped some lube into his palm then rubbed his hands together. He wrapped his fingers around Landry's straining cock before giving it a couple of tugs.

"Fuck, fuck, fuckety fuck." Landry squeezed his eyes shut. He was so close to coming it hurt but then Gage released him. Landry's dick bounced, almost hitting his belly. When he opened his eyes, he found Gage standing next to the bed, fisting his own hard shaft.

"Not fair!" Landry couldn't even see properly because Gage still wore his briefs.

"Don't worry, it'll be your turn again in a few minutes."

Landry groaned. "How long are you going to keep this up?"

"Sir."

"Sir. How long are you going to keep this up, Sir?"

"Well, that depends on how contrite you are for what you did this morning. I don't recall an apology." He slapped Landry's dick. "And you still won't get to come."

"I'm sorry?"

"Well, you don't sound too sure about that, sweetheart." Gage switched his focus to Landry's cock. This time he ran his thumb over the tip, pressing his nail into the sensitive slit. Landry jerked his hips, raising most of his body off the bed. Gage immediately let go of him.

"Aargh! You bastard... Sir."

"You might want to consider being a little more polite. I can keep this up all night." He slapped Landry's dick again.

"I'm sorry!" Landry wailed. "I promise I won't do it again."

This time Gage squeezed and stroked Landry's shaft for a full five minutes, never hard or fast enough to allow him to come. Landry tried to stay quiet in an attempt not to betray how close he was to orgasm but Gage gave him a knowing smile then released him once more.

"No!" Landry drummed his heels on the bed.

"Good subs don't have tantrums." Gage, who had slipped his hand inside his underwear once more, glared. He stripped off his shorts before climbing onto the bed where he knelt across Landry's thighs. He flicked Landry's cock with his finger, hard enough to sting, then did it again and again.

Landry yelped. "That hurts!"

"It's supposed to." Gage reached for Landry's balls, letting them settle on his palm before squeezing, applying steady pressure.

Landry didn't dare move or complain. The slight hurt made him want to come even more. He worked the plug in his ass with desperation.

"You look like you might be able to come without me helping you along," Gage said. "We can't have that."

He shifted his position so that he knelt inside Landry's spread legs then hoisted Landry's calves onto his shoulders, bending him back. He removed the dildo with care. Landry ached to be filled again.

"Please... Need you in me, Sir." Landry tugged at the cuffs attached to the waist belt.

Gage moved so that the tip of his cock teased Landry's entrance. He paused to glove his shaft before slicking it with more lube.

"Please! I'll do anything..."

"Anything, huh?" Gage drew circles on Landry's belly, leaving a glistening pattern of lube.

"Sir!"

Gage pushed forward so that just the tip of his cock entered Landry's body. "So hot." Gage moved far too slowly for Landry's liking, but there was nothing he could do but pray that Gage would give him what he needed. Gage thrust once, sliding deep, nudging Landry's prostate. Then he stilled.

"No, no, no." Landry muttered a selection of expletives under his breath.

"Such a dirty mouth. Perhaps we should stop while I gag you."

Landry clamped his lips shut, shaking his head frantically.

Gage chuckled. "You're enjoying yourself far too much."

Landry pouted.

In response, Gage jacked his hips without warning. He pistoned in and out of Landry's channel, harder and harder. Desperate to come, Landry sobbed his frustration. Gage reached between their bodies to grasp Landry's cock. One sharp tug was all it took. Landry's vision blanked and he came hard, screaming through his release, body jerking. Gage grabbed Landry's hips, holding him in place while he thrust into him a few more times. Muscles cording, he came, lips slightly parted, eyes shining. Landry had just enough awareness to know that he wanted to be responsible for putting that expression on Gage's face again and again.

Gage pulled free then leaned forward for a long, slow kiss. "Let me get rid of the condom then I'll be back."

Landry lay there, limp as a noodle, with a huge smile on his face. When Gage returned, he removed the cuffs and belt, dropping them down the side of the bed. He cleaned Landry up a little with some wipes, nudged him to one side then lay next to him, pulling the covers over them both.

"Just because your hands are free doesn't mean you're allowed to touch."

Landry snuggled close, soaking up Gage's warmth. "Yes, Sir. I mean no, Sir. I mean… I don't know, you've turned my brain to Jell-O. Strawberry flavor, because that's my favorite."

"Your mind is a fascinating place," Gage murmured. "I hope you have sweet dreams."

Landry closed his eyes. "They can't fail to be the best dreams ever."

* * * *

Landry started work the next day with a spring in his step. He was tired, but it was a good kind of tired and he couldn't seem to get the smile off his face. Gage had left early, but not before mutually satisfying blow jobs. It was almost better than coffee. Almost. The day kept improving because Prisha, Landry's friend from the Eastern Emporium across the street, had shown up mid-morning with two take-out cups of latte and a bag of freshly made samosas. Landry had eaten three and caught Prisha up on all his latest news, including a few unsubtle hints about Gage and details of his adventure with the Yakuza.

Not that it was that much of an adventure, really. I'll bet Gage has more excitement in five minutes than I get most days.

It was a dull day that started dry but developed into something wet and miserable in the afternoon. The rain began around four, darkening the sky enough that Landry had to turn on extra lamps in the store. By five the monsoon showed no signs of abating. Landry hadn't seen a customer in an hour and the street was deserted when he peered out of the window. He didn't mind. He'd had a good morning for sales — enough to make target and then some and, despite frequent paranoid glances outside, no strange cars had parked anywhere close. Gage had texted twice, using strings of strange emojis that Landry guessed the detective didn't understand.

Landry took advantage of the quiet spell to empty the jewelry cabinet and give it a good clean. He was a bit of a magpie and loved trying on the rings and bracelets. The most expensive item, an antique gold and diamond ring, was priced at over a thousand dollars, but it wasn't his favorite. That honor fell to a more modern ring, a flat silver band designed for a man that had a narrow strip of inlaid mother-of-pearl. It fitted Landry's middle finger perfectly, but he couldn't afford it and it would take years to save up enough money to buy it. Still, when he put everything back into the newly polished cabinet, he made sure to hide it at the back, where only the most curious of customers might spot it.

He locked the cabinet then took the key back to the cash register, where it lived most of the time. Another hour had passed and it was now fully dark. Landry could see the rain in the amber glow of the streetlights and where it bounced in puddles on the slick sidewalks. He doubted he'd see any more customers that day.

He ambled to the small kitchen area where Mr. Lao kept a kettle, one he'd brought back from a trip to the UK. Landry boiled some water then made himself a mug of instant hot chocolate from a packet. It wasn't as good as he could make in his apartment, but it was sweet, hot and better than nothing. His hands were chilly so he wrapped them around the mug before taking his seat behind the register to daydream about Gage.

A few minutes later and only halfway through his drink, Landry was surprised to hear the bell above the shop door jangle. Three men came inside. One of them turned the 'open' sign to 'closed' and flicked the catch next to the handle. He waited by the door while the other two marched down the central aisle. Landry's stomach knotted.

"I'd say can I help you, but I don't think you're here to buy anything, are you?" He took a few steps back.

"Where is it?" The man who spoke had cold eyes and a shaved head.

"Where's what?" Landry had no idea why he was engaging in conversation.

"Don't play dumb."

Landry sidestepped the man that lunged for him, noting that his hair and the shoulders of his jacket were wet. He dived for the aisle to the right then sprinted the length of the shop before twisting through a narrow gap between the piles of furniture into the next aisle. He dropped to his knees then crawled under a table into the corner near the jewelry cabinet.

"There's nowhere to hide, you little fucker. The harder you make this, the more it's going to hurt in the end."

All Landry could think was that the longer he hid, the more chance there was that someone might come by the shop, see the closed sign and suspect something was wrong. It was a very slim chance. Footsteps were getting closer, so he edged past the cabinet, squeezed around a bookcase then wiggled between a cast iron fire surround and a trench art umbrella stand. There was a slight clang as his hip caught the edge of the surround and it was enough to attract unwanted attention.

"He's down there."

"Cut him off!"

Fuck. Landry scrambled for the next aisle, knocking over a stack of walking sticks as he went. He grabbed one, rounded the next corner only to discover that he'd worked his way into a place where there was no escape other than back the way he'd come. His exit was now blocked by one of the men, his colleague close at his shoulder. Landry brandished the walking stick.

"Get away from me."

Shaved head grabbed the end of the stick, yanking Landry toward him. Landry let go and momentum made the man stagger backward, cursing. Landry dropped to the floor, then crawled through his attacker's legs. He yelped as the walking stick came down on his back.

"Grab him!" The second goon managed to get a hold of Landry's top, but he pulled away. The fabric tore, leaving his shoulder bare. He lurched to his feet then skidded around the corner, but in his haste to get away had forgotten the third man guarding the door. He was the size of a grizzly bear and when Landry ran into him, not looking where he was going, he may as well have run straight into a brick wall.

"Oof." Landry lost his balance and, arms flailing, fell onto his ass. The grizzly picked him up, slung Landry over his shoulder then carted him down the central aisle, where his colleague had positioned a chair. Landry found himself dumped on it like a sack of potatoes. Dazed, he had little strength to resist as his legs were taped to the chair. His arms were pulled behind it and taped at the wrists. He glared at his captors.

"Feisty little shit, aren't you?" One of the men backhanded Landry across the face, the force tilting the chair back. It rocked into place and Landry spat blood. The grizzly ambled back to the front of the store. The other two men stood in front of Landry. Despite his fear, Landry tried to take in as many details as possible. All three men were, he guessed, Japanese. Well-dressed and cold-eyed. None of them had drawn a gun, but he could see the tell-tale bulge of holsters beneath their jackets.

"Well?" Landry spat the word out. "What the fuck do you want?"

"Show some respect." The man standing to one side hit Landry again. He wore a heavy ring and the blow made Landry's vision blur.

"It's simple." His colleague, the one not getting his hands dirty, spoke. "All you have to do is give us the key. Then we'll leave you alone and you can get back to doing whatever it is you do in this mausoleum."

"I have no idea what you're talking about. What key?"

"You can act innocent all you like, but we know it's here. We know you have it, so tell us where it is before we tear this place apart."

"You want me to soften him up a bit more, boss?" The second guy flexed his hand and his knuckles cracked. The metallic taste of blood coated Landry's tongue.

"I'm afraid my friend here has a taste for violence. He does love to inflict pain but I'll give you one more chance. Tell me where the key is or I walk away and let him do what he will for the next ten minutes."

"I can't tell you what I don't know," Landry snapped. "The only keys we have in here are for the doors on some of the furniture. You can search all you like — you won't find anything because there's nothing to find."

The shaven-headed thug drew a hunting knife from the inner pocket of his jacket. He removed it from its sheath and Landry couldn't help but stare at the enormous serrated blade. "You think he'll get more talkative when I start carving pieces off him, boss?" The goon with a taste for blood grinned. Landry tensed. He worked his wrists, trying to loosen the tape. His tormentor pressed the tip of his index finger to the point of the blade, drawing a spot of blood. "Time's up."

Transfixed, Landry couldn't take his eyes off the knife as it was laid against his cheek. He guessed that even if he had known what his attackers were talking about and presented them with a gift-wrapped key, they would still have their fun. He leaned away but the pressure of the blade didn't change.

A huge crash split the silence and the sound of shattering glass drew everyone's attention to the front of the store. "Gage!" Landry prayed that his hero was coming to the rescue. He strained to see what was going on. The two men with him ran to aid their accomplice, who was flat on his back on the floor. Curses and yells filled the air. As the fight continued, Landry tore at his bonds. He managed to rip his wrists free then bent to tackle his taped ankles, all the while trying to keep an eye on the action. As soon as he was free, he ran for the cash register and the shelf where he stashed his phone. He dialed nine-one-one and gave a garbled explanation to the operator. A single gunshot had him ducking behind the counter where he hid, shaking. The noise stopped and, for a moment, an eerie quiet filled the store. Then there was the crunch of footsteps in broken glass.

"It's safe. You can come out now." The British accent told Landry that it hadn't been Gage who had saved him.

"You!" Landry hauled himself to his feet.

"A simple 'thank you' will suffice." James Ellery wiped his bloody nose with the back of his hand. "I do believe I'm going to have a black eye." He wandered over to the nearest mirror, peering at his reflection.

"What are you doing here?" Landry asked.

"Hauling your pretty little backside out of trouble, it seems."

"But that's not why you came by, is it?"

"I told you I didn't give up easily." Ellery smirked. "I was going to give asking you out on a date another try. I saw the 'closed' sign on the door and knew it was too early. I guessed you may have snuck out to buy a coffee and as it's raining cats and dogs out there, which I have to say reminds me of England, I decided to shelter in the doorway until you came back. The gorilla guarding your door gave me a clue that something was amiss."

"Amiss? Who talks like that?"

"Anyway, the gorilla attempted to wave me away and I took exception to his attitude. A shoulder to your door was all it took to break it down. Poor security by the way. Fortunately, the bigger the gorilla, the harder he falls. To be fair, I think he hit his head on the way down and was dazed. Then his chums joined the party and things got interesting."

"I heard a shot."

"They missed me."

Sirens sounded in the distance. "About time," Landry muttered. "Then what? You offered them a cup of tea and they declined the invitation?"

"I guess they realized they weren't going to get what they wanted and cut their losses. They ran, but not before they got in a few lucky punches. I don't suppose you have a steak, do you? Or a bag of frozen peas?"

Landry shook his head. "I think I have a frozen pizza upstairs."

"I don't think that's going to be much good for my eye." Ellery grinned.

"Oh, I wasn't thinking."

"No, really?"

"Hey, sarcasm is *my* thing."

"You don't have the monopoly."

"I suppose I should thank you."

"You can thank me by accepting my invitation. Come out for a drink with me."

Landry stared at the handsome blond. He did look kind of dashing, splattered with blood, his eye swelling. "No! I told you before, I'm with Gage."

"Tempted though, aren't you?"

"Am not."

"Are so. Your face is a bit bashed too—are you okay?"

"I'm…" Landry prodded the multiple sore bits of his face. "I don't know what I am."

"What the hell were those guys doing here anyway? They weren't robbing the place, were they?"

"I have no idea." Landry knuckled his temples. "But I'm beginning to wonder if there is a side to Mr. Lao I don't know about, though he's never been anything but honest and kind. Perhaps it was a case of mistaken identity." The sirens got closer and blue flashing lights strobed the store.

"It seems I must be going." Ellery blew Landry a kiss. "Another time."

"Wait!" Landry called after him, but Ellery had already gone. *That man has an annoying habit of disappearing.* Landry braced for the interrogation he knew must come, wondering how his day had gotten so bad so fast.

Chapter Eleven

Landry sat on his chair behind the cash desk and watched, helpless, as a bunch of people trampled through Treasure Trove. Every time a booted foot crushed broken glass, he winced. *Mr. Lao is going to kill me. In fact, he's gonna think that death would be an easy way out. He's gonna torture me, then kill me, slowly. My feather duster is gonna end up in a place the sun don't shine.* Landry sagged, exhausted. He was cold and longed for a coffee. The two cops who had questioned him half an hour earlier, before telling him to stay put, were at the front of the store talking to a woman who Landry guessed must be a crime scene tech. The broken door allowed gusts of cold, damp air to sweep down the center aisle directly to where Landry sat and shivered. He wondered how long it would be before he could make arrangements to get the door fixed. His phone, which he'd put on silent, vibrated. He'd had text messages from almost everyone he knew on the street, all wanting to know what was going on, and asking if he was okay. He kept his responses short, knowing that they'd all be around to find out more once the cops had departed. He sniffed, holding back tears.

Raised voices at the front of the store drew his attention. "Gage." Bemused, Landry watched Gage berate his colleagues. Landry couldn't quite make out what was being said, but from Gage's gestures, he wasn't pleased. When he was done, the two cops made their way outside and Gage stalked down the aisle to where Landry sat. He came to a standstill with his hands on his hips.

"I can't leave you alone for five minutes, can I?"

Not trusting himself to speak, Landry shook his head. His lower lip trembled.

"You're shaking. You're in shock and you're injured. I can't believe those idiots didn't look after you better. If I have my way, they'll be on traffic duty for the rest of their miserable lives."

Landry managed to smile, though it didn't last. "They're just doing their jobs and I only have a few bruises."

"Don't defend them. I'm gonna make sure their asses are written up at the first opportunity. You're a victim and at the very least you should have been seen by a paramedic instead of being left to sit here in the cold."

"You think you might be a little biased?" Landry slipped off his chair and took a few halting steps around the cash desk.

Gage frowned. "No. Maybe. It doesn't matter. I'm taking you upstairs to your apartment where you can tell me everything that happened." He pulled Landry into his arms.

"But the door," Landry protested. "I have to get it fixed."

"It's all under control. We have a firm on call." Gage held him tighter.

"I don't know whether to be grateful or worried that this happens so often you have a guy on retainer."

"Upstairs, Landry."

"Fine." Once Gage loosened his hold, Landry made his way to the door between the store and the hall then trudged up the stairs and into his apartment, Gage close behind him.

"Go park your behind on the couch, while I make some coffee," Gage said. "And don't even think about arguing with me."

Landry didn't have the energy to fight. He made his way to the couch, slumping into one corner. He grabbed a cushion to hug, kicked off his shoes then drew his knees up in front of him. The events of the day played over and over in his head like a film reel stuck on repeat.

When Gage appeared, coffee mugs in his hands, he took the chair rather than the couch, placing the drinks on the coffee table. "I'm sitting here because if I get closer, I'll either want to kiss you or spank you. Probably both. And I have to stay a detective for a while rather than the lover who just wants to hold you."

"What did I do?" Landry whined.

"You have marks on your face and arms. I'd guess they are going to turn into bruises and I wouldn't be surprised if there are more under your clothing. Your lip is split and swollen and you've been crying. That doesn't make me feel good, Landry. I wasn't here and I should have been."

"How could you be? None of this was your fault. You have a job and I'm a grown-up."

"This is my case. After you spotted the car lurking outside I should have arranged protection for you."

"Stop it! I don't need your guilt on top of mine. Mr. Lao left me in charge and so far it's been a complete car crash. He's gonna kill me, then fire me."

"That makes no sense whatsoever." Gage's serious expression broke into a grin. "And he's not going to blame you either—he'll understand. You've been incredibly brave."

Landry grabbed his coffee then resumed his position, wishing he were in Gage's lap instead. "Why is this happening? I haven't done anything. I don't get why anyone should be after me when I'm just a not-too-bad sales assistant in an antique store."

"Tell me what happened. Every detail, Landry, however insignificant it might seem to you."

Landry related the day's events in as much detail as he could, hoping he remembered everything. When he got to the part where James Ellery had arrived, Gage's eyes darkened. Landry ignored his expression and carried on to finish his story. "I still don't know what key they were talking about. There are dozens of keys in the store..."

"Did you tell Ellery about the key stuff?"

"No. Why would I? I have no clue what it meant."

"I think I may be able to shed some light on that. Wait..." Gage pulled out his phone, which had started buzzing. "It's my partner." He answered the call. "Hey, Sancha. Sure, come on up. Top floor." He put his phone on the table. "She's on her way. She was on the street talking to witnesses."

"There are witnesses?"

"Only to the three men getting away. No one seems to have seen them arrive. They had a vehicle parked down the street, far enough away that you wouldn't spot it and get suspicious."

"It was raining when they showed up and the street was quiet. I hadn't had a customer in ages, so I'm not surprised there weren't many people around."

Gage grunted. "Let me get the door for Sancha. Don't move."

"Where would I go?" Landry sipped his coffee, curious to see what Gage's partner would be like. She arrived before Gage, tossing her bag on the floor by the couch.

"Two sugars in that coffee, Gage," she shouted in the direction of the kitchen.

"You think I don't know that?" Gage yelled back.

Sancha rolled her eyes. "And you must be Landry. Sancha Hernandez. Gage is my partner in crime. I'm the boss, of course."

"Of course." Landry shared a grin with Sancha. *I like her already.*

"Well, I can see why Gage has been getting his tighty-whities in a twist over you."

"He doesn't wear any," Landry retorted.

"I like you." Sancha took a seat next to Landry. "How you doin', sweetie? Don't suppose the big lug bothered to ask?"

"He did, kinda. I'm a bit bewildered. Scared. Mad." It was easier to open up to Sancha somehow.

"Mad is good. I'd be mad if three moronic thugs had invaded my place of work. Those look sore."

Landry's wrists jutted from his sleeves displaying the red welts left by the tape he'd been bound with. He shrugged. "They tied me to a chair with tape. Had to rip it off."

She reached over to rub at one wrist with her thumb. Her hands were cool. Soothing. "And your poor face… They roughed you up some."

Landry gripped his mug tighter. "Yeah. I was lucky."

"I won't ask you to go through it all again. Gage can fill me in."

"Can I ask if you learned anything from the witnesses?"

"Other than the direction the perps drove off in, afraid not."

Gage returned, took one look at Sancha's position on the couch and frowned.

"Gimme!" Sancha held out a hand for her coffee. "Landry and I were getting to know each other."

"Oh God." Gage resumed his previous seat.

"We're gonna be pals."

"Fuck."

Sancha smirked. "Now, how about you tell Landry what we found at the warehouse scene?"

"I was about to before you showed up demanding refreshments."

Landry looked from Gage to Sancha then back again. "You two are better than a sitcom. In fact, you could be one."

Gage gave a pained sigh. "We'll discuss suitable friends for you later. In the meantime, what my esteemed colleague is referring to happened at the operation the other night. At the raid on the warehouse…"

"The one where you got yourself shot?" Landry asked.

Sancha snickered.

"Yes, that one. We recovered silver and paintings, no jewelry, but in one of the dead guys' pockets there was a slip of paper."

"Wait. What? You didn't mention dead guys. What the hell went on that night, Gage?" Landry's voice rose.

"Not relevant. The words 'find the key' were written on a note we found."

"So everything's linked. We *are* going to talk about the dead people, Gage, I haven't forgotten, but crap—why on earth do these people think I have something to do with all this? I don't understand."

"That's what we have to work out."

Sancha patted Landry's knee. "Don't you worry, honey. From now on we're gonna look after you better."

"How?" Landry was close to tears. "I can't close Treasure Trove."

"And we don't want you to," Sancha said. "But you won't be alone. We are going to give you a new assistant."

"Are you gonna work in the shop?" Landry thought he could handle that.

Sancha giggled, the sound making her seem younger. "Not me. Gage."

"Oh!" Landry chewed on a fingernail.

"Stop that," Gage said. "As of tomorrow, I'll be working with you at least for the next few days. Someone out there is getting impatient. I don't think we've seen the last of your Yakuza friends and I'm not having you bait a trap alone."

Sancha got to her feet. "I need to get home. Landry, it was a pleasure. Try to get a decent night's rest, okay?" She gave him a hug. "And you." She waggled a finger at Gage. "No keeping him up all night. I assume you'll be staying?"

"I'll be here." Gage stood. "I'll follow you down to lock up." He glanced at Landry. "Don't get into any more trouble while I'm gone."

Landry rolled his eyes. "I'll try not to."

Gage was gratified to find that work on securing the shop's front door had been completed. Wooden boards covered the parts that should have been glass but replacing the panes would take longer. Inside the store, someone had swept up the broken glass and apart from the boarded door, it was impossible to tell that any violence had happened. He locked the door between the shop and the hall then went outside to deal with the security shutter. On the way back he locked the gate onto the road, thinking all the time that none of the security arrangements were safe for Landry to be handling alone, even in normal circumstances. With a grunt of dissatisfaction, he secured the hall door and, with an excess of caution, pushed a tin bucket and mop in front of it. Muttering to himself, he stomped up the stairs, latching Landry's apartment door once he was inside.

"Why does your boss not have an alarm system?" he asked Landry, who had pulled a fluffy throw over himself.

"He doesn't like technology. Have you seen how old the cash register is? He only switched from an antique one with keys because he got fed up of writing out receipts, and he still keeps a ledger. If you want to give him a lesson in security when he gets back, be my guest."

"You're pale. Do you have any cooking supplies?"

"Sure. I can't afford take-out all the time."

"Stay put. Nap if you want to. I'll throw something together."

Landry's eyes grew big and round.

"Don't look at me like that. I can cook some."

"I didn't say a word." Landry blinked.

"You didn't have to." Gage retreated to the kitchen to explore the cupboards and the fridge. He found the makings of mac and cheese and decided that comfort food would be a good option. He set the pasta to boil before making a cheese sauce from scratch. Once it was ready he mixed the two together in a casserole dish. Humming to himself, he created his signature topping by combining panko crumbs, parmesan cheese, melted butter and paprika. "Perfect." He sprinkled the mixture over the top of the pasta then pushed the dish into the oven before walking through to the lounge. Landry was watching baseball on the TV.

"That won't take long. I'm impressed you had panko and parmesan," Gage said. "I didn't know you were a sports fan." He sat next to Landry.

"Oh, I'm not."

"Then why…?" Gage gestured at the screen.

"They wear super-tight pants, obviously. Football isn't bad, but I prefer baseball. Or wrestling!" Landry's eyes lit up. "Lycra is my friend. I also like diving, swimming, gymnastics…"

"I get the picture." Gage shook his head.

"You have a great body too."

"Well, thanks. I think."

"You do! That six-pack is a thing of beauty and you have gorgeous thighs, and calves, and your chest is…"

"Stop! I won't be able to eat the mac and cheese at this rate."

"Why not?"

"Because I'll be worrying about my calorie intake."

Landry chuckled. "I think you can stand a bit of carb-loading."

"You can help me work it off later."

Landry blushed, the color making him look a bit healthier. He twisted the corner of the throw in his hands.

Could he be any more adorable? Even if he is a brat. "Come here." Gage pulled Landry onto his lap. "You've had a tough day and I made it worse by interrogating you. I'm sorry."

"At least you didn't tie me to a chair...actually, that wouldn't have been so bad...with you, I mean, not the Yakuza guys."

"No one should be putting marks on you except me." Gage rubbed Landry's wrists.

"They'll be gone by tomorrow, then you can replace them, Sir."

"Sounds good."

"Hey!" Landry bounced in Gage's lap. "I've just realized...tomorrow I'm gonna be your boss!"

"In your dreams."

Landry pouted. "But you'll be working for me — that means I'm in charge."

"I think you'll find that I could be scrubbing floors for you but *I'd* still be in charge."

"Oh, that's... You're making me hard."

"Dinner first. Playtime later."

"You're spoiling me, Sir."

"After what you've been through today, you deserve it, but it won't happen often. I'll get our food." Gage lifted Landry off his lap. He had a smile on his face all the way to the kitchen. It was time to step away from being a detective and give Landry some comfort and care. He couldn't think of a better way to spend the evening than with Landry, good food and a night's cuddling to look forward to.

Chapter Twelve

"I never imagined you'd have so many customers coming in and out of here," Gage said. "People buy the weirdest stuff."

"Hey! That weird stuff you're talking about is antique. Every piece has history. Imagine what a seventeenth-century armoire may have witnessed."

"It's an inanimate piece of furniture. It didn't witness anything."

"You're thinking like a cop. You need to discover your romantic side." Landry shifted on his stool, grimacing.

"Uncomfortable?" Gage grinned.

"What do you think?"

"I think I'm enjoying watching you squirm."

Landry stood, and the plug in his ass shifted. He worked the invader with his inner muscles, hoping no one could see what he was up to. There were still a few people browsing the aisles and Gage's knowing grin was a giveaway. Landry muttered curses under his breath. The leather strap Gage had buckled around the base of Landry's balls was tight and getting tighter by the minute.

"You're mean."

"That's not what you were saying this morning, when I put the plug in," Gage said.

Landry's mind went back to the scene in his bedroom. Him on his hands and knees on the bed, legs spread. Gage fingering his hole, driving him wild with need then pushing the thick rubber plug into place. Gage hadn't let him come, just buckled the strap, smacked Landry's rump and ordered him to get dressed.

Landry sighed. *It was perfect, but I'm not telling him that.*

"You know you're smiling, right?"

"I am not." Landry pressed his lips together in a tight line. *God, he's infuriating... And gorgeous... And, fuck, I'm a lost cause.*

Gage smirked. "What would you like me to do, boss?"

Landry could think of a few things involving cuffs, floggers and a lot of lube but none were suitable for public consumption. "You could give the storeroom a good dusting. I put a load of new stuff in there the other day and it was all pretty dirty. I haven't cleaned in there for a while."

"What do you keep in there?"

"Stuff that hasn't been valued yet, things waiting to be repaired or restored, stuff that Mr. Lao thinks might sell better in specialist auctions, that kind of thing."

"I don't like leaving you out here alone."

"Prop the door open and you'll be able to see me," Landry said. "There are cloths and dusters on the bottom shelf. To be honest, if you're back there it won't be so obvious that I've got a bodyguard. That's better for the investigation, isn't it?"

"Good point. Shout if you need me." Gage ambled over to the storeroom.

Landry surveyed the aisles, checking out the current batch of customers. He had a vague feeling of anxiety, something he wasn't used to, and he found himself examining each person with suspicion. He didn't think any of them looked like the types to be involved in organized crime but looks could be deceptive. Who was he to know whether the old guy with the handlebar mustache and silver-topped cane wasn't an international arms dealer, or if the woman with a sleeping baby strapped to her chest in a carrier was a hard-core drug dealer? He shrugged. *There's no point in worrying.* He wandered over to an elderly couple admiring a glazed, oriental pot stand, to offer his assistance.

An hour or so later, Gage emerged from the storage closet with dust in his hair and a dirty smudge across his cheek.

"When you say you haven't cleaned in there for a while, how long are you talking about?"

Landry gave him a sheepish grin. "I lose track of time, so I can't be sure."

"Anyone around?"

"Not at the moment, the last customer just left."

"Good." Gage pushed Landry over the cash desk then gave his backside six swift slaps. Landry yelped as the plug nudged his prostate over and over again. His cock jerked and strained. "That's for knowing full well how filthy it was in there." Gage whirled Landry around then kissed him hard.

"Do that again!" Landry was a little breathless and far too turned on, but the entrance bell jangled and a group of people walked in. "Damn." He brushed the dust out of Gage's hair then handed him a tissue. "You have dirt on your face. After that, I think the least you can do is go get me a coffee. I don't think a bunch of old ladies are going to do me any harm."

Gage rubbed his face. "I'm not leaving you here alone, old ladies or not."

"But I need coffee!"

"I *will* get you a coffee, but only because I want one too, and not until the local patrol guys show up." He leaned closer. "Tomorrow, I'm going to make you wear nipple clamps under your shirt."

Landry gulped and fixed a smile on his face as an octogenarian with a blue rinse approached him, clutching a pair of brass candlesticks.

Once the patrol car was idling outside, Gage left for supplies. He didn't take long and he was whistling when he returned, clutching two tall take-out cups of coffee. He waited until Landry had finished serving the customer he was dealing with before handing over the drink.

"The glass guy just pulled up outside."

"That's good," Landry said. "A boarded-up door isn't the most attractive invitation to prospective customers."

"You could have fooled me." Gage slurped his coffee. "I'd bet half the people who have been in here today only wanted to ask you about the broken door."

Landry *had* given his fictional explanation for the damage several times. "I'm grateful for the business. I'm going to have enough explaining to do when Mr.

Lao gets back without having crappy sales to show him too."

"I was thinking while I was in the coffee shop," Gage said.

"Careful now, you could strain something."

"You just guaranteed no orgasms for the rest of the day and you're going into chastity tonight. To get back to what I was saying, I wanted to ask you about some of the things in the storeroom. There's a whole bunch of stuff that looks oriental. Did that come in recently?"

"Yes, it did. You remember that crate you moved the other evening from Mr. Lao's nephew, Eddie? All that stuff was in it."

"Remind me, where did it come from?"

"A neighbor of Eddie's who passed away. Mr. Lao valued some stuff for the family. The old lady's grandson dropped the box off with Eddie to bring over here."

"Is Eddie's surname Lao?"

"Yes, he's Mr. Lao's brother's son. Why?"

"What about the neighbor's grandson, do you know his name?"

"No, I've no idea. I suppose Eddie would be able to tell me."

"Don't ask him yet. I need to do some checking first. Is there any other way you could find out?"

"I could text Mr. Lao. He might know but he doesn't look at his phone that much so I'm not sure how long it will take him to reply. He'll want to know why I need the information too. What do you want me to tell him?"

"How about that you found something in the box that didn't belong there and you need to get the grandson to come and collect it?"

"Okay, that should work. I'll do it now."

"Thanks. In the meantime, I'll call Sancha and get her to check up on Eddie."

"Am I allowed to ask where this is coming from?"

"Think about it. For some reason, some very nasty people think you have information about an item they want. This item is of significant value and they're not likely to give up until they get it. You took receipt of a box of oriental antiques shortly before all this trouble started. I'm guessing there has to be a link to the key."

"This is crazy."

"I could be completely wrong, but I don't like coincidences. I'm gonna find a quiet spot to make my calls. When you get a chance, can you give those pieces a good look over and see if you can spot anything unusual or out of place?"

"I can have a go," Landry said. "But I'm not an expert. You need Mr. Lao."

"Have a look anyway. There may be something that sticks out to you that I would never spot."

"Okay, I'll do it later, when it's quiet."

Landry spent the rest of the afternoon itching to get into the storeroom, but a steady stream of customers meant that he couldn't leave the cash desk. When the patrol car came by, Gage made a couple of short trips to get lunch and another coffee but spent most of the time talking on the phone. It was still nice to have someone around and, when Landry had to take a toilet break because of all the coffee, Gage proved able to charm the customers until Landry returned. Gage even allowed Landry to take out the plug, about ten seconds before Landry thought he would have to use his safe word. By early evening, the store was deserted. Landry was just about to head to the storeroom when Gage gestured to him.

"I need to go out. I don't know if I'll be back tonight so I want you to close early and lock everything up before I go. I want you safely upstairs in your apartment and you have to promise me not to go out."

Landry debated arguing, but the look on Gage's face told him it would be a worthless exercise. He would only be closing an hour early and the circumstances were exceptional.

"I can see you're trying to think of a reason not to do what I'm telling you, but I'm not taking no for an answer, Landry. Either you lock up then head upstairs or I carry your disobedient ass up there myself then take all the keys away."

"You make a persuasive argument," Landry said. "I'll do it because I don't want to be here alone, but no chastity."

"You drive a hard bargain."

"It's non-negotiable. If you're not gonna be around, I have to be able to amuse myself."

"The no-touching rule still applies."

Landry gave him a slight smile. "Of course... Sir."

Gage shook his head. "When this mess is over, and it will be over soon I hope, I'm putting you into a strict training regime."

"I..."

"No, no speaking. You'll just dig yourself into an even bigger hole. Not that I don't have an endless supply of suitable punishments for you."

"I never got a chance to look at that stuff in the storeroom." Landry decided a change of subject was in order.

"It can wait until tomorrow. If I'm not back by morning, don't open. You wait for me, understand?"

"Yes, Sir." Landry gave Gage his best pleading look. "But come back tonight if you can. I don't care how late it is." He detected a slight flush on Gage's cheeks. "And stay safe. No getting yourself shot again."

Gage pulled him close and treated him to a long, inspiring kiss. When he finally pulled away, he left Landry breathless and gasping. "Let's get this place locked up. Really should extend that to you too."

* * * *

Once Gage had gone, Landry headed straight for the bathroom. Working in an antique store wasn't exactly manual labor but he still managed to get filthy. He took a shower, resisting the urge to jerk off, then made himself a quick supper of grilled cheese and soup. He felt the need for comfort food, even more so because he was alone. Gage's absence was strange. They hadn't been together long but Landry needed his Dom.

Wow. I have a Dom! Landry experienced a brief moment of panic but it was soon replaced by a slow warmth spreading through his body and something inside him settled into place. He wondered if Gage felt the same about their relationship, not that Landry would dare ask him. The more he let that thought play around in his head, the more he needed reassurance. He could use a distraction. Gage hadn't told him he couldn't go back to the store and everything was locked up so he'd be safe enough. While it was quiet, he could take the opportunity to give the new oriental stock a good look over.

Landry padded down the stairs, wearing his Cookie Monster slippers. They were oversized, so he had to be careful not to trip, but they kept his feet warm and with the heating off in the store, the stockroom would be cold. He unlocked the door between the hallway and the store then made his way to the back of the shop. In the dim light, the scent of old furniture was even stronger. Landry breathed deeply. He loved the sense of age that came with the smell. There was a pull cord inside the storeroom that lit a bare bulb, which was so bright Landry blinked and his eyes watered. He examined the shelves full of artifacts. Gage had done a good job cleaning and tidying everything—the whole room was much more ordered than before.

"Control freak," Landry muttered with a smile. "He's even domming the antiques."

He decided to follow Gage's example and replace his usual scattered approach with something more methodical. Starting at the top shelf, he worked his way down, examining each piece in turn. He didn't really know what he was looking for, but he shook each object with care, listening for a rattle from any possible secret compartment. He ran his hands over the surfaces, seeking fine breaks or cracks that might conceal an opening. To his semi-expert eyes, everything looked as it should. Other than a hairline crack in one vase that he made a mental note of, he didn't find anything out of place. There was certainly nowhere to hide a key. With a sigh, he turned off the light before walking across the store. He almost jumped out of his skin when Gage appeared in the connecting doorway.

"Holy crap, you scared me." Landry took a few calming breaths.

"What in the ever-loving hell are you doing down here?" Gage asked. "I should chain your wandering ass to the bed."

"I missed you. I was thinking too hard. I needed to do something and I guessed it would be safe enough down here. Don't be mad with me."

"Tell me you at least had your phone with you." Gage did not look happy.

"Um…" Landry scuffed the toe of one fuzzy slipper against the floorboards.

"What am I going to do with you?" Gage held his arms open and Landry walked into them.

"Cuddle me? Kiss me some?"

"I should be punishing you. I want you to be safe, that's all." Landry tilted his head back, hoping for a kiss. Gage brushed his thumb across Landry's lips. "Your sense of self-preservation is nonexistent." Then he kissed him. "Come on, I could use a coffee and I have some news for you."

Once they were back upstairs and settled on the couch with mugs of coffee, Landry gave Gage an expectant look. "So tell me. You got back much earlier than I expected you to, so you weren't on another stakeout. I didn't find anything in the stockroom. Not that I knew what I was looking for, but everything seemed normal."

"That's a shame," Gage said. "Sometimes the obvious solution to a problem is the right one, but not in this case. I'm surprised because it relates to what I've got to tell you. Firstly, I've had people doing some digging into the background of James Ellery. It seems he is who he says he is, at least on the surface. He's a self-employed investigator working mainly for insurance companies who handle high-end art, luxury goods, antiques and jewelry. He has a decent find rate for stolen property, though the people we talked to at the company he does most work for admitted that some of his methods could be considered dubious. He's paid commission on the value of the finds on top of travel expenses. No salary, so his income depends on his results. I still don't trust him, but he's not top of my hit list anymore."

"He was top of your list?"

"He was. You have to admit his behavior has been suspicious and he's only shown up here when you've been alone."

"Is he dangerous?" Landry asked.

"I'd say he could be," Gage responded. "I certainly don't trust him with you."

"That's so cute." Landry preened, basking in Gage's overprotectiveness.

"Says the man wearing Cookie Monster slippers."

"They were a present from my mom, okay? She always called me Cookie Monster when I was a kid because whenever she baked I'd hover around the kitchen to get the first ones out of the oven. I've always had a sweet tooth."

Gage gave a low chuckle. "I bet you were a handful."

"I did act up a bit. Took advantage of being the youngest. My two brothers are four years older than me and they beat up anyone who messed with me at school and my mom spoiled me. She still does."

"I won't... Spoil you. I mean."

"No, really? Color me shocked."

"Brat."

Landry wiggled. Gage's rough tone had the inevitable effect of plumping his cock. "What else did you have to tell me?"

"If you stop squirming, I'd be able to concentrate on what I'm saying."

"Sorry?"

"Remember what you told me about the crate of stuff that came in on consignment?"

"The stuff I was looking through? Sure. Mr. Lao did some valuations for the family of his nephew's neighbor. Once things with the estate were settled, the lady's grandson dropped the box off at Eddie's place. He delivered it when he had the chance."

"You'll be glad to know that Eddie is in the clear but the grandson is a different matter. We tracked him down and got a name. Tadanobu Tsukamoto has a juvenile record and is known as a runner for the Yakuza. Low-level stuff, but definitely connected."

"Oh, wow." Landry wasn't sure what to say. "Have you got him in custody?"

"He's done a disappearing act. We'll find him eventually, but that's not the point. It could explain why you are a target. There may have been nothing in that box but it seems our criminal friends don't know that. They think you're in possession of this key and Sancha and I believe that the key leads to the missing jewelry from the robbery in Japan."

"Which also explains why James Ellery is so interested. But wait, how would he know that this Tsukamoto guy is involved?"

"I'd guess a man in his position has plenty of underworld contacts. Interestingly, I also found out this evening that the tip-off we got for the raid the other night was phoned in by a man with a British accent."

"Wouldn't he have disguised his voice?"

"Why would he bother? The tip was anonymous, the call was too short to be traceable and likely came from a burner phone anyway. I think it was him. I also think he knew we wouldn't find the jewelry, but that we might get a lead from the guys we arrested."

"And you did. The note about finding the key."

"The pieces are starting to come together."

"So why do you look so worried?"

"There are dangerous players in this game, Landry. If I'm getting closer to finding the jewelry, they are likely to up their efforts to get to it first."

"You think they'll be back?" Landry drew up his knees and hugged them.

"They'll try to get to you somehow. Try not to worry. I'm not gonna leave you alone."

"Pinky swear?"

"Promise."

Chapter Thirteen

Gage was glad he had taken the time to go home and pack a few extras in his overnight bag. Landry needed to be taken away from his worries and Gage was happy to make sure Landry had nothing on his mind but sensation.

"You are stunning."

Landry couldn't answer with more than a mumble, the bit gag made sure of that, but his eyes sparkled in the lamplight. Gage stroked the back of his hand along the inside of Landry's thigh, enjoying the twitch of muscles beneath his touch. Landry was stretched taut, arms and legs extended in a star shape. Gage had used supple leather cuffs on Landry's wrists and ankles, their baby-blue color perfect against Landry's skin. A wide spreader bar kept his legs apart while his wrists were chained to the headboard. His cock was firmly secured in an acrylic chastity device—the key on a chain around Gage's neck.

"I do enjoy touching you." Gage had been indulging himself for the past half hour, exploring Landry's body, teasing his nipples but, so far, avoiding his groin. Gage had stripped to his underwear, his boxer briefs tented and straining to contain his erection. He wanted inside Landry's sweet body. He also wanted to hear Landry's whimpers and squeals. He removed the gag, wiping traces of saliva from Landry's face.

"Watching me drool not one of your fetishes?" Landry asked.

"No, but seeing your frustration while I fuck you in chastity is." It was hard for Gage to keep a straight face as he watched Landry's expression of disbelief. "You didn't think I was going to let you out, did you?" Landry pouted. His glistening lips were too hard to resist so Gage leaned in for a kiss. "Tomorrow, if you're obedient, I might be persuaded to release you."

"Tomorrow! That's so long…I wanna come!" Landry whined.

"Complaining will just add hours to the time you're locked up."

"I…yes, Sir."

"That's better. Good submissives listen to their Doms." Gage stripped off his underwear and Landry gasped, his eyes comically wide.

"Am I your submissive? I mean…I was thinking earlier that I have a Dom, but then I worried that maybe you didn't feel the same. I don't even know if you want your own sub."

After a pang of guilt that he hadn't been clearer, Gage cleared his throat. "You're mine, Landry. Don't forget it. My submissive. Mine to direct, to pleasure, to punish."

Landry's smile lit his entire face and inside, Gage glowed. He'd made his submissive happy and that was as good a rush as any narcotic could ever manage. If

Landry's contented sigh was anything to go by, he was just as happy. Gage fondled Landry's balls. "Hot."

"And blue," Landry muttered.

"You want me to gag you again?"

"I thought you wanted to hear me scream?"

"Good point. Never let it be said that I don't listen to my sub." Gage removed the spreader bar, leaving the cuffs around Landry's ankles. "Pale blue leather suits you. I like black but this makes a nice change." He massaged Landry's insteps, admiring his slender, delicate feet. "And these are much improved without the hairy slippers."

"If you keep insulting my Cookie Monsters, I might have to safe word."

"Well, we can't have that. I'll note it as a hard limit." Gage fought to hold back his laughter.

"You do that." Landry dissolved into giggles and Gage followed with a belly laugh that shook his whole frame.

"And on that note, I think it's time we got to the serious stuff, don't you?"

"If you say so, Sir."

Gage gloved his cock then slicked it with an ample quantity of lube. "You want me to go easy?"

"You remember how long I had that plug in for today, don't you?" Landry rolled his eyes. "I'm more than ready for you."

"Good. Because I'm about ready to pop. I don't think I could take this slow if you paid me a million bucks."

Landry snickered. "You have a nice collection of cock rings — why don't you use one of them on yourself?"

"Brat." Gage clambered onto the bed, pushing Landry's legs apart so that he could kneel between them. He hoisted Landry's calves onto his shoulders then edged closer, bending Landry back. "Good thing you're flexible." He targeted Landry's hole with his cock then pushed forward in one smooth motion. "Fuck. You are bad for my self-control." He grabbed Landry's hips, raising his ass off the bed so that he could slide in deeper. From that point on he had to be selfish. He took what he needed, using Landry's body without mercy. A few hard thrusts and his orgasm rolled over him in waves. He filled the condom, wishing there were nothing between him and Landry. Shuddering, muscles trembling, he thrust a final time, milking the last few drops of cum from his body. Shattered, he withdrew. He rolled to one side to avoid crushing Landry. "Fuck, that was good."

Landry rattled his chains. "How about you let me go so I can give you a hug?"

"I was going to leave you like that all night but a hug sounds good." Gage unfastened the chains, leaving the cuffs in place. "Cuffs and a smile is a good look on you." Landry rolled into Gage's arms, sprawling across him. "Give me a minute to get rid of the condom."

"Don't be long." Landry gave him enough room to get out of the bed. Gage made a quick run to the bathroom, wanting nothing more than to get back to the warmth of Landry's body and the snug bed. Once under the covers, he pulled Landry close. "How do you feel about getting tested?"

"You wanna go there?"

"Yes." Gage had never been more certain of anything.

"That would be amazing. I never have... I've never trusted anyone enough."

"We can go together. There's a clinic that opens in the evenings."

"Don't you get tested because of your job?" Landry asked.

"Yes, but I think this is something we should do together."

"That's...so sweet. There's a real soft center beneath that tough cop exterior, isn't there?"

When it comes to you. "Don't let it get out," Gage said.

"How about you let me come and I promise not to tell Sancha?"

"How about you don't tell Sancha and I don't spank you so hard you can't sit down?"

"I suppose."

"And the cuffs stay on tonight."

Landry kissed Gage's shoulder then nibbled his way up his neck until he could reach his lips. Landry tasted of coffee and mint. Bittersweet.

"Thank you," Landry murmured.

"For what?"

"For making me forget."

"It was my pleasure."

"It certainly was," Landry said, his tone wry.

"Go to sleep, Landry. Have happy dreams. That's an order from your Dom."

"Yes, Sir."

* * * *

Landry awoke warm and contented. The weight around his wrists and ankles made him smile, the weight around his cock not so much. Next to him, Gage snuffled. Even in sleep his forehead was creased. *Worrying about me, about everything.* Landry glanced at

161

his shelf of lucky cats. *Grant me some of that luck now!* He slipped beneath the covers, burrowing his way toward Gage's dick. It was stuffy and dark but Landry found his target with the instinct of a homing pigeon. He began with a few gentle licks, grinning as Gage's cock awoke before the rest of his body, coming to full hardness with little prompting. *Someone's horny this morning.* Landry decided against a slow tease and instead plunged his mouth over Gage's shaft, taking as much as he could in one go. He sucked hard, savoring the salty taste, then repeated the action several times, eliciting some imaginative cursing from Gage. Landry paused. "You're awake then?" Gage stroked the bits of Landry's body he could reach in response, coming to rest on his head where Gage tangled his fingers in Landry's hair.

"Don't stop," Gage ordered.

Landry was quite happy to obey. He went back to work, determined to give Gage as much pleasure as he could. He sucked until his jaw ached and Gage's thighs trembled.

"Fuck!" Gage came in a hot stream down Landry's throat. Landry swallowed, enjoying every drop. He licked Gage clean, spent some happy time nuzzling his balls then crawled up his body to emerge from beneath the covers.

"Good morning!"

"It certainly is."

Landry straddled Gage's body, the covers pooled around his hips. His dick, locked in plastic, rested on Gage's chest. Landry looked from it to Gage and back again. He didn't dare ask to be released.

"Because you didn't ask..." Gage remove the keychain from around his neck. He undid the device, removing it with care. Landry's cock sprang to attention and he groaned, desperate to come. Gage tumbled him onto his back, looming over him. Then he did what Landry had done to him, but better. Landry lasted brief seconds before he came so hard that stars twinkled in front of his eyes and he felt a little dizzy.

"Oh... My... God."

"A religious experience, then?" Gage chuckled.

"I think I'm going to found a new cult, the order of the orgasm."

"Should prove popular." Gage rolled to one side. "What time is it?"

"Time for you to treat me to something better than Lucky Charms for breakfast. The coffee place next door does the most amazing pastries."

"I don't suppose we have time to go to a diner? I'm craving bacon."

"No, we don't. But I'll get a pack out of the freezer then I can cook for you tomorrow morning. You are staying again tonight, aren't you?"

"If work doesn't get in the way."

"I should go shower." Landry would much rather stay in bed. Mr. Lao often opened the store so that Landry could have a slower start and he was missing that part of his usual routine. Mr. Lao preferred to finish early and let Landry close up.

"When your boss gets back, and you can take a couple days off, I'm gonna hide you at my place. Fuck you senseless."

"Sounds dreamy. Will you take me to the club too?"

"Sure. I want to show you off and let all the local Doms know you're taken."

"I love it when you get all Dommy and possessive," Landry said. "I suppose these have to come off." He fiddled with the buckle on one wrist cuff.

"I think your clientele might be a bit shocked if all you wear to the store are cuffs."

Landry rolled around laughing. "I suspect some of my old ladies might enjoy it more than they should. I've had my ass slapped a few times. They have no shame."

"I'm not against arresting senior citizens," Gage growled. "Your butt is mine. I should put up a notice."

"Yeah, that would work."

"Go shower. I'll slip out for some breakfast then take my turn when I get back."

"Don't forget the coffee."

"What if I bring you some nice herbal tea instead?"

"Because you want to live to see your next birthday?" Landry scampered for the bathroom.

Within the hour, he and Gage had been through their bathroom routines and munched their way through a bag of cherry and apricot Danish. Landry had downed his coffee then gone downstairs to sort out the float for the till and check over the store. He sent Gage for a second round of coffees the instant he spotted the patrol car parking outside. Gage had them taking their breaks nearby, and he always bought them coffee too.

Gage unlocked the security shutters on his way back, coming into Treasure Trove through the front door. He deposited Landry's coffee on the cash desk. "You must keep that place next door in business. They know me now. I don't even have to tell the barista my order."

"Coffee is ambrosia. It is the meaning of life and I have to take advantage of you being here. When I'm on my own, I suffer greatly."

"I know how to punish you then, don't I. Ban you from drinking coffee for a couple of days."

"You wouldn't?" Landry's horror wasn't faked. "That kind of cruelty is against the Geneva Convention."

"And you're not allowed to use your safe word over a cup of coffee."

"You're evil."

"If I chained you to a wall then drank the coffee in front of you—that would be evil." Gage smirked.

Landry huffed and grabbed his duster. "You can watch the desk while I take my frustration out on cleaning."

"Sounds good. I have a few calls to make, but I'll look forward to the day when I have you cleaning my place in nothing but a collar."

It was difficult to walk with an erection. Landry needed to find a quiet spot where he could calm down and think deflating thoughts.

It proved to be an uneventful day in the store. The weather, which showed early promise, turned around midday. The skies darkened and rumbles of thunder preceded driving rain. The customers stayed away and Landry took the opportunity to do some updates to the store's website, which he'd created himself. There were even a few online orders to dispatch, which he wrapped and labeled ready for a courier to collect.

Apart from a brief run out to get sandwiches for lunch, Gage spent most of the day attached to his phone while keeping a watchful eye on the door and casting suspicious glances at the few customers who had come in before the weather broke.

Landry parked his butt behind the cash desk. "How about we go out for something to eat this evening? I'm getting a bit stir crazy."

"Sounds good. Do you have anywhere in mind?"

"Don't cops know all the best places to eat?"

"There's a small mom-and-pop Italian place I like. It's near my neighborhood so I go there quite a lot."

"I love Italian food." Landry thought he might drool. "And they always make amazing coffee."

"In that case, I'll lock up while you go change."

Landry skipped up all four flights of stairs. Tired though he was, the thought of a date with Gage gave him renewed energy. Their relationship so far had hardly been normal and though Landry wasn't enamored of normal at the best of times, after the last few days he'd be very content with being boring for a while. After a quick shower, he changed into a pair of soft jeans with a strategic rip across one thigh and his only, precious cashmere jumper, which was a shade of royal blue. As it was still raining, he opted for boots rather than his usual sneakers and he dug a raincoat out of the closet, more to protect his sweater than anything. He waited in the living room while Gage took his turn in the bathroom, emerging clad in thigh-hugging black jeans and a cream cable sweater. Landry wanted to jump him right there and then.

"You look edible and your pullover is made to be snuggled." He jumped into Gage's arms, wrapping his legs around Gage's hips.

"You clean up pretty well yourself." Gage kissed him, his lips hot and sweet.

"You taste of toothpaste."

"Then we're both minty fresh, aren't we?"

Reluctantly, Landry stood on his own two feet. "I'm ready. Shall we go?"

"Let me grab my coat," Gage said. He slipped his holster on before putting his jacket over the top.

"That's kinda scary."

"Just forget it's there and enjoy the evening. I have something for you."

He drew a length of coiled leather from his pocket. It was pale blue, like the cuff set Landry had worn.

"Is that…?" Landry trembled with excitement.

"It's a collar." Gage slipped the narrow band around Landry's neck, clipping it shut at the back. "Not too tight?" He tested the fit by running a finger underneath it.

Landry shook his head, for once unable to find the right words.

"Hey, it's okay… You've earned it, you know. This one can't be permanent because you'll have to take it off to shower. Doesn't make it any less meaningful."

"I never thought… I mean… I'm a little overwhelmed right now." Landry touched the supple material. "They won't mind at the restaurant?"

"Not at all. You may even recognize the owner from Scorch. Be warned, he doesn't have a sub at the moment and he has the softest heart of any Dom I've ever met. He'll probably want to adopt you."

"I think I like him already," Landry said, relaxing. "You're smiling."

"I tend to do that when I'm happy. I've been saving that collar for a long time. I was beginning to think I'd never find a man worthy of it."

Landry's face heated and he cast his eyes down. "I'll be the best sub I can be for you."

"You should be you. Nothing more. Nothing less. Now, I'm starving. How about we make a move?"

Determined not to cry, Landry rubbed the back of his hand across his eyes. Not trusting himself to speak, he nodded, then followed Gage from the apartment, letting him do lock-up duty at each door they passed.

Gage's Jeep was parked on the opposite side of the street and Landry ambled across the road while Gage was still dealing with the padlock on the yard gate. It was darker than it should have been, even in the rain, and Landry realized that the streetlight nearest to Gage's parking spot was out. There were shards of glass in the gutter. Landry shook his head, wondering why even the most bored teenager would bother aiming rocks at the light. The passenger door of the Jeep was curb-side so he waited next to it for Gage to join him.

There was a screech of brakes and the smell of burning rubber as a car skidded to a halt in the middle of the road. Wild-eyed, Landry froze as two men brandishing guns leapt out and made straight for him. He yelled. Gage was already halfway across the road. For an instant, Landry's brain stopped working. He didn't want to do anything that would put Gage in danger, but he couldn't stand there like a dummy while he was attacked. He dropped to the floor, then rolled off the curb to the only available hiding place, under Gage's jeep. Water soaked through Landry's jeans and gravel grazed his hands as he crab-scrambled sideways toward the road where he could see Gage.

"Stay there!" Gage shouted, throwing himself behind another vehicle.

"Fuck." One of the gunmen fired two shots toward Gage's hiding place. "I'll cover you. Drag the kid out!"

Landry scuttled back and forth, keeping away from where he could see boots by the side of the Jeep, avoiding the occasional curse-accompanied grab. There was a shot, then another… Landry hunkered down, put his arms over his head and prayed. He heard scuffling, swearing and the sound of running feet.

"Seattle PD. Stop or I'll shoot." A woman's voice issued the command. After more gunfire, two car doors slammed and a vehicle screeched away.

His heart pounding, Landry didn't dare move. *Please let him be fine. Please, please, please.*

"They've gone. You can come out now, Landry." Gage sounded tense and angry. Landry rolled back toward the pavement then scrambled clear of the Jeep. His clothes were filthy and sopping wet. Gage rounded the car then pulled him into a tight hug. "Are you hurt?"

"No." Landry pressed his face against Gage's jacket. He was shaking uncontrollably. "What about you? They didn't get you, did they? There was shooting. I hate guns!"

"Morons couldn't hit a barn door at three paces. Their shots went wide. I think I got one of them in the leg. Fuck, they took one hell of a risk trying to grab you off the street."

"They were after me?" Landry went cold. Gage held him tighter.

"Put him down, Gage." Landry recognized Sancha's voice. Reluctantly, he stepped away from the security of Gage's arms.

"Hi, Sancha. What's up?"

"One of these days, Landry, we're going to meet under better circumstances." Sancha gave him a hard squeeze. "You okay, big guy? I was a bit slow getting to you."

"You were here when it mattered," Gage said. "I'm not sure they would have been scared off if I'd been the only one with a gun."

"Pulling your ass out of the fire again, huh?"

"Yeah, yeah, if it makes you feel better, you can think that."

"I called it in, so the cavalry will be here soon."

"Wonderful," Landry said. "The way things are going I'm gonna get run out of the neighborhood for causing so much disturbance." There weren't that many residences in the area but one or two people were standing on the street rubbernecking. "I suppose I'm not going to get my nice Italian dinner now, either?"

"Not tonight, sweetheart." Gage squeezed his shoulder. "How about once we're done with the uniforms, Sancha and I take you to our favorite diner instead?"

"Okay." Landry sat on the curb, picking bits of gravel out of his palms while Gage and Sancha conferred. He sniffed, wrinkling his nose, wishing he had a tissue.

"You told me you weren't hurt," Gage accused, standing over him.

"I'm not," Landry protested. "It's just some scrapes." He held his palms up for Gage to see.

"You're bleeding."

"Honestly, Gage... It's nothing. They just need cleaning up and some antiseptic ointment or something. I am wet and cold, though. Would it be okay if I go in and change? My pants aren't fit to be seen in public."

"Sure." Gage walked him across the road, undid the gate then the door into the building. "You have your keys?" Landry nodded. "Then I'll lock up behind you and deal with things down here. They're gonna need a statement from you too."

"I won't be long."

"The collar stays on, Landry." Gage's tone brooked no dissent and it gave Landry a much-needed warm feeling as he ascended the stairs to his apartment. His pants went straight in the laundry hamper. He hung his coat on the back of the bathroom door because it would have to go to a dry cleaner. His sweater had survived its adventure unscathed, so Landry settled for clean jeans and a fleece hoodie because he didn't own another coat. He gave his hands a thorough wash, checking them as best he could for embedded dirt before smearing on a layer of antiseptic gel. The grazes were sore but not deep—he'd had much worse in the schoolyard or when playing with his brothers as a kid. He'd left his wallet and phone on the bed so he went to retrieve them. Inside the bedroom door, he stilled, staring. With a shuddering breath, he gave himself a smack on the forehead.

"You stupid fucking idiot." He reached for the most recent acquisition in his lucky cat collection. Running his fingers over its body, he discovered a seam around its middle, well disguised by the intricate pattern. "Gage is gonna kill me, spank me then kill me again. I can't believe I forgot about this." Clutching the cat, he raced down the stairs, across the yard then out into the street after a brief fight with the lock.

"Gage!" Landry yelled.

"What? What's wrong?" Gage hurried across the road from where he'd been leaning into the open window of a cop car.

"I'm so dumb." Landry thrust the cat toward Gage.

"Why are you giving me a china cat?"

"It's not china, its porcelain, but that's not the point!" Landry could hardly get the words out. "This was in the crate."

"Slow down. What crate? What are you talking about?"

"The crate that came from the grandson via the nephew to the hall. The one you put in the corner."

"You're not making a whole lotta sense. Wait…you mean the crate with all the oriental stuff?"

"Yes! How many other crates have you lugged around recently?" Landry snapped, his frustration getting the better of him.

"Inside. Now." Gage waved his partner over. "Sancha, ask the guys to hold on, will you?"

"Sure." Sancha chatted to the cops in the car then trotted over to join them. She didn't ask questions, just followed Gage and Landry inside. "The guys will keep an eye out."

Gage opened the connecting door to the shop and they all gathered around the cash desk.

"There's a break in it," Landry said, putting the cat on the desk. "It's been repaired, I think. It already had a broken ear, that's why I added it to my lucky cat collection but when I went upstairs I realized it's Japanese, not Chinese like the rest of the stuff that was in the crate. It didn't belong with the other stuff. I doubt it came from the same place."

"Holy moly," Sancha muttered. "Break it open, Gage."

"There's a small hammer in the drawer," Landry said. "I use it for knocking odd nails back into place."

Gage got the hammer out, examined the cat then laid it on its side. He gave it a gentle tap with the hammer and it fell into two parts. "There's nothing inside," he said, sounding disappointed. "No key."

"Damn it!" Sancha added.

Landry picked up the bottom half. "But look at this!" He turned the base so that Gage could see the inside. "I don't think Japanese artisans scrawled numbers in Sharpie inside their creations."

"Six digits. Well, fuck. The 'key' is a code or combination, not a physical key. You found it!" He pulled Landry and Sancha into a three-way hug.

"I did, didn't I? But what does that mean?" Landry was elated but more confused than ever.

Chapter Fourteen

It didn't take Gage long to come to the conclusion that he and Sancha would have to go into work. "I'm sorry, Landry. We can't do the research we need to on phones. We need PD resources and secure computers. Our dinner will have to wait. I can get you some take-out before we leave."

"Don't worry about it. I won't starve. There's a frozen pizza in the freezer and I've got some salad and stuff. It's much more important that the two of you get to work and find whatever that key code opens. Those idiots won't come back now… Will they?"

"I doubt it very much," Sancha said. "One of them was injured and they will have realized that we were waiting for them. They won't risk it again, not tonight anyway."

"I agree," Gage said. "I still don't like leaving you here on your own. The patrol car will be here a while and I'll ask them to cruise past every now and again through the night."

"I'll be fine," Landry insisted. "I don't want to be the reason this case drags on. I want it over just as much as the two of you do."

"If you're sure…" Gage leaned in for a kiss.

Sancha fanned herself. "Did it get hot in here?"

"I should make you turn your back," Gage said.

"Get lost, the two of you," Landry admonished. "I have a date with my onesie and a bucket of hot chocolate." He ushered them out of the store then headed up the stairs while Gage locked doors behind him. Landry's steps were dragging by the time he reached his door. He'd kept a cheerful face on for Gage, but he was sad and a little anxious to be left alone. He decided to get as cozy as possible, then find some hunky sportsmen to watch on the TV.

Half an hour later he was cuddled in the corner of the couch with a plate of pizza, a mug of steaming hot chocolate and a bowl of chips. He'd found European soccer on the TV, which was enough to keep him amused for a while. His panda onesie was warm and he'd pulled the hood up for additional coziness. A fleecy throw across his lap meant that he was as contented as he could be under the circumstances. Gage had texted to let him know that he and Sancha had arrived at the station and that they were getting to work. He'd promised to text again if they found anything interesting.

Landry finished his food and chocolate, the milky drink making him drowsy. He lay out on the sofa and drifted into a doze, imagining what it might be like when he and Gage finally made it to Scorch for an evening. The snug fit of the collar around his neck made him feel loved. It crossed his mind that he did love Gage and that jerked him into wakefulness.

"Holy crap! This is what being in love feels like." He closed his eyes again, a smile on his face.

He wasn't sure how long he snoozed but he woke suddenly, thinking that he'd heard a loud noise. He wasn't sure and whatever it was didn't happen again, so he told himself it had been a dream. His bladder told him it was time to visit the bathroom, so he made a quick trip, dumping his dirty plate and mug in the kitchen sink on the way past.

In the bathroom, he did his business then splashed some water on his face. He wasn't sure whether to go to bed or wait up for Gage. A yawn overtook him, making his mind up. He grabbed his phone to check the time. It was after midnight and there had been no second text from Gage, so Landry sent a short message saying that he was turning in, following the words with a heart emoji. He was just about to climb into bed when the buzzer from the street gate sounded. He jumped, his heart pounding, then laughed at his own reaction. It was probably someone on their way home from a bar or club, thinking it was funny to lean on the buzzer. He stood waiting for a minute or two, but then it sounded again.

"What the hell?" He wished, not for the first time, that Mr. Lao had installed an intercom rather than just a buzzer. There was no way Landry was going down and unlocking the doors without knowing who was there. He left his apartment and crossed the landing to the only window he could easily access with a view of the street. It was around the corner from the front gate but if he shouted, whoever was there should hear.

"Who is it?" he yelled.

There was no answer but then a familiar figure came into view. Even in the dim light, the blond hair was a giveaway.

"Landry, it's me, James Ellery."

"It's after midnight. What are you doing here?"

"I got into a spot of bother. I'm injured and I didn't know where else to go. I need help."

Landry cursed. Gage would probably kill him, but he couldn't leave James out on the street. "Go back to the gate. I'm on my way." He grabbed his keys then made his way out to the yard and across to the gate. The rain had slowed to a drizzle, but it was cold and Landry shivered. He wasn't wearing anything beneath his onesie.

"Why are you dressed as a panda?" Ellery asked before Landry could even open the gate.

"None of your business," Landry snapped. "Is there anyone else around?"

Ellery glanced up and down the street. "No, no one. And hey, if you're into the furry stuff, that's fine. Each to his own."

"I am not into the 'furry stuff', as you put it." Landry pulled open the gate. "Get in here."

Ellery limped into the yard and Landry quickly locked the gate. "How badly are you hurt? My first aid is sketchy, to say the least."

"I'll live."

"Do you need to go to a hospital?" Landry half shoved Ellery into the hall so that he could close and lock the door.

"No hospitals. I don't need well-meaning doctors and nurses asking questions I don't want to answer."

"I hope it's not too bad, because I'm not carrying you up four flights of stairs." Landry marched up the first flight, hoping that Ellery would be able to follow under his own steam. He was far too big to carry.

Ellery trudged slowly up the steps, his face pale and drawn. He had to stop and take a few deep breaths on each landing but they eventually made it to Landry's apartment. Landry guided him to the couch. "Sit."

Ellery dropped into place with a groan.

"Tell me what happened." Landry stood facing him, hands on his hips, fully aware that it wasn't possible to look stern while wearing a panda onesie and Cookie Monster slippers.

"Like I said, I ran into a spot of bother," Ellery said. "I don't suppose I could trouble you for a glass of water, could I?"

Landry stomped to the kitchen to fetch a drink. When he returned, Ellery had his shirt off. Landry stared—he couldn't not look at smooth skin and sculpted muscle—but his gaze was soon drawn to the livid bruising down one side of Ellery's body. He handed over the glass of water. "That looks painful."

"I'd like to be stoic and say it isn't, but it hurts like a bastard."

"So did you tangle with a moving vehicle or did a person do that to you?"

"Well, strictly speaking, the damage was done by a baseball bat, but there was a person wielding it at the time."

"Are your ribs broken?"

"No. At least I don't think so. He only got me twice."

"You are fairly obnoxious, but I wouldn't go so far as to say you deserve a beating. I have some Tylenol…" Landry ran to the kitchen to fetch the tablets. "Would you like anything else?" he shouted from the kitchen.

"No… Pills would be great, but then I should be on my way."

"Where are you going to go?" Landry asked.

"Not sure. I'll find some anonymous hotel, then hunker down for a couple of days, I suppose. I think they've been following me and it's likely they know where I've been staying. Don't worry, I made sure I wasn't followed — and what's with all the police action around here? Avoiding the patrol cars took some doing."

"Seattle PD are diligent. Who's *they*?"

Ellery gave Landry a hard look. "I'm not sure I should tell you."

"You want these painkillers?" Landry waved the packet.

"Blackmail?"

"Normally I'm quite fond of the strong, silent type, however, on this occasion my curiosity overrules common sense."

"Fine, but if I tell you, it goes no further."

"I don't keep secrets from Gage."

"I can see that. The collar is a recent acquisition, isn't it?"

"That's none of your business."

"For what it's worth, he's a very lucky man. It suits you. I should have liked… Never mind. I had a bit of a run in with the Japanese mob."

"You mean the Yakuza?"

"Of course, you're familiar with their activity. That's who I rescued you from the other day, isn't it?"

"More familiar than I would like to be, and yes, it was them," Landry said, handing over the pills. "Is that why you were attacked, because you helped me?"

Ellery gulped down three tablets, finishing his glass of

water. Landry watched his Adam's apple move as he swallowed.

"I've no idea but I'd guess so. Not sure how they could have tracked me down but they have a long reach."

"I assume you're not going to go out without your shirt on?"

Ellery smirked. He shrugged into his discarded clothes then stood with a wince. Landry sighed. "For fuck's sake. I can't believe I'm saying this, but you can stay here tonight. On the couch."

"I couldn't put you to that kind of trouble."

"It would be more trouble for me if I threw you out into the night because I wouldn't be able to sleep for worrying."

"You'd worry about me?" Ellery grinned.

"Yes, because I'm a human being and not a complete douchebag." Landry went to the linen closet to fetch a pillow and blanket. "You should be warm enough with these." He laid them on the arm of the couch. "I'm going to bed. I'll text Gage to let him know you're here because there's a chance he may come back in the night."

"I consider myself warned."

"If you stray from that couch, just remember my boyfriend carries a gun."

"Noted."

"The bathroom is down the hall if you want to use it. I need to sleep. It's been one hell of the day."

"I appreciate this," Ellery said. "I won't forget it."

Landry grunted then ambled toward his bedroom. He lay on the bed with his phone, thinking how best to text Gage. He ended up writing, 'the Brit is on the sofa, don't shoot him.' Less than a minute after pressing Send, the phone rang.

"Care to give me an explanation?" Gage's tone was mild, but Landry wasn't fooled. The irritation was evident in every word.

"He showed up here, injured. He was beaten up by the Yakuza... At least that's what he told me. I've seen the damage, so someone definitely got to him and probably because he helped me out in the store the other day. He offered to leave, but I couldn't throw him out. I told him he could sleep on the couch."

"Your kind heart will get you into trouble one of these days."

"As long as I'm not in trouble with you," Landry said.

"Not for being a good Samaritan, though I still don't trust that Brit. You know they play the bad guys in all the best movies, don't you?"

"That's not a good reason for distrusting an entire nationality."

"I like the Brits just fine, just not the good-looking ones with the hots for my boyfriend."

"He does not!"

"How could he not?"

"He spotted my collar. He knew what it meant."

"That doesn't surprise me in the least. I'll be there in an hour or so. If his ass isn't firmly attached to the couch, I may have to shoot him, just for fun."

"Fine, but don't get any blood on my rug, 'kay?"

"I'll see you soon, sweetheart." Gage hung up, leaving Landry with a warm feeling in his belly. He'd worry about the clash of the alpha males when it happened.

* * * *

Landry woke when Gage started fiddling with the zip on his onesie. He batted at Gage's hands. "Whatcha doing?"

"Much as I like the furry costume, I guess you fell asleep before you undressed as you're still on top of the covers, rather than under them. I was about to unwrap you."

"Okay. Is the Brit still alive?"

"Don't know. Don't care. There was no movement from the couch, so I came straight in here."

"Good. I don't have much in the way of expertise when it comes to disposing of dead bodies."

"I'm relieved to hear it." Gage went back to dealing with the zipper, wrestling with the panda suit until Landry lay naked on the bed apart from his collar. "I think this is how you should dress all the time when we're alone."

Landry was still half asleep. "But I'm not dressed."

"Exactly."

Landry giggled before maneuvering himself beneath the comforter. "Are you going to stand there all night or get in here and fuck me?"

"I thought that collar might make you feel a bit more submissive, but that streak of brat is still strong, isn't it?" Gage stripped, dropping his clothes where he stood.

Landry shrugged, wriggling deeper beneath the covers. "Then you'll just have to suck it out of me, won't you?"

"Who gives the orders around here?" Gage got into bed then rolled Landry onto his belly.

"You do, Sir."

"Try to remember that. Get on your hands and knees."

It was the work of a moment for Gage to glove and lube his cock. Landry shivered. He rested his forehead on crossed arms. He couldn't wait for Gage to be inside him. Gage pushed a finger into Landry's hole, then added another. The prep was quick and efficient. It felt good, but Landry craved Gage's thick cock. He didn't have to wait long.

"I don't want to hurt you, but I'm short on patience tonight."

"You won't... Please..."

Gage pushed home, nudging Landry's prostate as he did. He stilled for a few seconds and it was just enough time for Landry to get accustomed to the stretch and fullness. Landry pushed his ass back. He wanted Gage deeper. He got a slap across the butt for his trouble.

"Keep still, brat." Gage grabbed Landry's hips, digging his fingers in, holding him in place. He moved fast, snapping forward again and again, plunging deep into Landry's receptive body. Hard and aching, Landry gripped the sheets, trying to remain still. It was difficult to think or even to breathe as Gage pounded Landry's ass like it was the last time he was going to get the chance. With a final, powerful thrust, Gage came, pulling Landry back so that his ass settled against Gage's groin, his wiry hair tickling Landry's backside. Gage remained inside him and reached under Landry's body to grasp his dick. A few tugs and Landry spilled over the sheet, howling through his release. They collapsed in a pile on the bed, Landry squashed beneath Gage's weight until Gage rolled them both onto their sides. He hadn't yet withdrawn and was still semi-hard. Landry loved that they were still connected. He didn't want to get out of bed and managed to reach for a tissue to mop up the worst of the wet spot.

"Wanna sleep like this."

Gage pulled the discarded comforter over them. "Fine with me. Think we woke up the Brit?" He sounded smug.

"I forgot he was even there," Landry murmured. "But yes, I imagine we did." He smiled. Gage pulled him even closer, wrapping Landry in a prison made from Gage's arms.

"All mine."

"Caveman."

"Go to sleep, brat."

"Yes, Sir." Landry's fingers strayed to his collar and he drifted into sleep touching the leather.

Chapter Fifteen

Landry awoke to the scent of frying bacon. Eyes still closed, he reached across the bed to pat the space where Gage was supposed to be. Landry's hand met Gage's solid bulk.

"Go back to sleep, Landry."

"If you're still here, he's cooking." Landry cranked his eyelids open. "Ellery."

"What about him?" Gage sounded like he had gravel in his throat.

"I think he's cooking breakfast. I can smell bacon."

"Perhaps he's not such a worthless piece of crap after all," Gage muttered. "I'm hungry. Didn't get any dinner last night, just shared a bag of chips with Sancha." As if to demonstrate, his stomach growled.

"I'll go investigate." Landry grabbed sweats and an old T-shirt. Barefoot, he padded along to the kitchen where he found James Ellery cooking up a storm.

"Hey, Landry, I hope you don't mind. I found eggs and bacon and couldn't resist. It's been an age since I had a decent fry up."

"Make yourself at home."

"Sarcasm is part of your genetic makeup, isn't it?"

"Yes, though it has adapted and mutated over time. How long till I get bacon?"

"As soon as you tell me how many eggs you want."

"One for me, two for Gage. Over easy."

"Five minutes. Go lever the ape — I mean Gage — out of bed. Though I imagine he needs all the rest he can get after the amount of exercise he got last night."

"Protein for breakfast is good. He needs his stamina." Landry couldn't help wiggling his butt as he marched back to the bedroom. Gage was pulling on his jeans over a black jock, the elastic framing the perfection that was his ass. Landry licked his lips, sighing when denim covered all that deliciousness.

"Well, a night's sleep didn't make him any less of an asshole," he said.

"Why don't you take a quick shower, while Mr. Ellery and I get to know each other?" Gage's smile was wolfish.

"No breaking my dishes. I only have so many plates."

"I can play nice. Wait." Gage removed the leather collar from Landry's neck and replaced it with his St. Christopher. "A temporary solution — you should still consider it my collar."

Landry fingered the medallion, still warm from Gage's skin. "Thank you." He gave Gage a kiss then sloped off to the bathroom, hoping that he didn't come out to too much devastation. He washed and dressed in super quick time and when he was done, to his utter shock, he found Gage and Ellery sitting at his tiny dining table, conversing like grown-ups. His plate of food, still nice and hot, was waiting for him. He sat with Gage to one side and Ellery opposite him.

"Okay, so which one of you had a personality transplant while I was in the shower?"

"Have a bit of faith," Ellery said. "We have come to a mutually agreeable diplomatic solution. Conversation is limited to the weather, bacon and sightseeing in Seattle."

Gage nodded. "I was just about to tell James about the Fremont market."

Landry crunched on a mouthful of bacon. "Oh, that's so cool. It has loads of one-of-a-kind and vintage things, handicrafts, antiques — and you get to see stuff from new designers and artists. There are loads of street food vendors as well."

"Sounds like some of the European fairs," James said.

"I wouldn't know. I've never been to Europe." Landry squirted extra ketchup onto his plate. "There's Pike Place too, that's another market, and you should go up the Space Needle of course, the Museum of Pop Culture is great, and somewhere I haven't been but would love to go is the Chihuly Garden and Glass — another museum. It has this huge, one-hundred-foot-long sculpture suspended from the ceiling. It's all red, orange and yellow. I've only seen pictures, though."

"I'm not sure how long I'll be here," James said. "But those all sound like places I should look up."

For a few minutes, the conversation stalled while they chomped on their bacon and eggs. James and Gage finished first then Landry pushed his plate away last. "That was great. Food always tastes better when I don't have to cook it myself."

"Well, considering your usual idea of breakfast is a bowl of cereal or to send me next door to the café for pastries…" Gage rolled his eyes.

"It's not often I'm up early enough to eat this much before I have to start work," Landry said. "I like my bed too much." He gave Gage a sultry glance.

James cleared his throat. "And on that note, I think I've taken advantage of your hospitality for too long."

"Landry, could you give us a minute, please?" Gage's request was an order in disguise.

Landry considered complaining about being sent away like a child but decided against it. He went to clean his teeth and finish getting ready to open the store. When he got back, Gage and James were in the kitchen cleaning up.

"Still friends then," Landry observed.

"I've asked James to stay for the day," Gage said. "I can't be here with you and I don't want you alone in the store."

"And I've agreed." James winked. "Though I have been warned that if I even look at you wrong, parts of my anatomy that I'm quite fond of will be detached from my body then pickled."

"You two are unbelievable," Landry exclaimed. "I don't need a babysitter!"

"Yes, you do." Gage and James spoke in unison, then shared a conspiratorial grin.

"I give up. So long as someone keeps me in coffee and snacks, I don't care. Don't get in my way." Landry glared at James. "I wouldn't want a heavy piece of furniture to fall on you by accident."

"And here was me under the impression that you Americans had such friendly, welcoming dispositions."

Landry huffed. "If the two of you have quite finished trying to control my life, it's almost time to open."

"I'll take care of the security shutters on my way out," Gage said. "Remember what I said, Ellery. No matter how much he begs for coffee, you don't leave him alone unless there is a patrol car outside. They'll be by every hour or so."

James nodded.

"It's a fucking conspiracy," Landry muttered, stomping toward his apartment door. "Today is going to be the longest ever." Gage caught up with him on the landing and pushed him against the nearest wall.

"Behave yourself today, brat. You're wearing my collar, remember that, and if you have any trouble with blondie, text me and I'll come back and shoot him."

"What will you be doing?" Landry asked in between kisses.

"Sancha and I have the unenviable task of tracking down one combination in a city that has thousands of safety deposit boxes, banks, storage warehouses and property lockers. Narrowing down where your combination might be of use is a big job and you know I'd much rather be here with you. Ellery is injured and isn't going to be much use in a fight. I'm hoping that his presence alone will be enough to put off a return visit from our Yakuza friends. I've also arranged for the local beat officers to carry on with their drive by every hour and take their coffee break outside your door. Anyone watching should get the message not to mess with you."

"Good luck," Landry said, stealing another kiss. "Let me know how you're doing, won't you?"

"Oh, you can be sure I'll be checking up on you at frequent intervals. The Brit is far too polite to be trusted."

"You like him, don't you?" Landry suggested, grinning.

"I'm not going to credit that with an answer," Gage replied. "Now get to work."

"Yes, Sir." Landry stepped away from Gage to find James lurking in the apartment doorway, smirking.

"Have you two finished making out?"

"You really like living on the edge, don't you," Gage growled.

"It makes life interesting." James took the stairs slowly, his ribs clearly still bothering him, though he didn't make a sound of complaint.

Gage followed then Landry brought up the rear. He was looking forward to the sanctuary of old furniture and knickknacks. Most of his customers were at least semi-sane and much easier to deal with than two Dommy alphas. First order of the day would definitely be to send James next door for a triple shot latte. *With any luck, the cops will already be outside.*

* * * *

Thanks to a steady stream of customers, Landry managed to avoid being in close proximity to James Ellery for most of the morning. He set him a continual series of tasks and sent him to the café every time he spotted a cop car. By lunchtime, Landry had a pleasant buzz from an excess of caffeine and baked goods. Gage had texted twice with a series of nonsensical emojis, including an octopus and an erupting volcano. Landry decided both were open to interpretation.

"How do you manage to stay so thin?" James asked, depositing his latest purchases on the cash desk. "If I ate as many pastries as you, I'd be the size of an elephant."

Landry examined James' lean, toned form. He clearly had cast-iron willpower. "I'm blessed with good genes."

"And do you bleed red or coffee-colored? Your caffeine addiction is astounding."

"Is yours decaf?" Landry asked, narrowing his eyes in suspicion.

"What if it is?" James sipped his drink.

"You sound defensive."

"Guilty as charged."

"Decaf coffee should be banned as a crime against humanity." Landry gave a happy sigh as he sipped his vanilla latte. "What are we going to have for lunch?"

"Your stomach is a bottomless pit."

James sat behind the cash desk while Landry strolled the aisles chatting to customers. "Hey, Landry, what's with the broken cat?" he called.

Landry froze. He did a slow turn to see that James had retrieved the lucky cat from the shelf beneath the register. Landry hadn't realized it was still there. Gage had taken pictures of it, but Landry had assumed Gage had taken the cat with him for evidence. Hoping that his expression didn't give anything away, Landry went to stand beside James. "Oh, I'm going to attempt to repair it. I have a collection of lucky cats. It's not worth anything—I give a home to all the broken ones that come in."

James turned the pieces over in his hands. "You should be able to glue it. Seems like a clean break." He put the pieces back where he found them and Landry took a deep breath. "Are you okay? You seem a bit flushed."

"I'm fine." Landry wandered away. He wanted to grab the cat and hide it but didn't dare show any more interest in it.

The next hour crawled by. When James offered to fetch burgers for lunch after the patrol car showed up, Landry agreed with relief. He dealt with some customers while James was gone and the last one left just as James returned. To Landry's surprise, James set the catch on the door then turned the 'open' sign to 'closed'. He hurried down the aisle.

"I was followed. There are three of them, I think, and the cops left before I could get to them. Is there another way out of here other than the front door or yard gate?" He dumped a take-out bag on the counter.

Landry went cold. "Not again."

"Landry, the exit!"

"Oh... Yes. There's a fire escape at the side of the building. We can get to it from my apartment. It ends in the alley."

"Let's go."

As he and James ran for the door to the hall, shadowy figures appeared by the front window. With fumbling fingers, Landry locked the connecting door, then tore upstairs after James. Landry ran through his apartment to the kitchen window, the one which gave access to the fire escape.

"You go first," James said. "If I can't keep up with you, run. Don't wait for me."

"Run where?"

"Somewhere public. Then call Gage."

"I have an idea," Landry said. "When we're out, follow me."

Landry scurried down the iron staircase. The last section was a descending ladder, which fortunately Mr. Lao kept well maintained. It didn't make much noise as it slid into place and Landry dropped to the ground. The fire escape ended in an alley that ran the length of the street. Landry ran to the end, terrified that he would be seen. James caught up with him, his face drawn with pain.

"If you can find somewhere to hide," Landry said, "I know where I can get my hands on a vehicle."

"I'm fine. I'll come with you."

"Okay." Landry did a loop through alleys that led back to the street, though further along than the store. Keeping low behind parked cars, he made his way to the Eastern Emporium. Inside, the stock was a riot of color and multiple scents competed for air time but for once Landry wasn't distracted. He spotted his friend Prisha in the fabric section. Her eyes widened when she saw him.

"What happened to you?"

"Long story, Prisha. Can I borrow the van? I'm in trouble and I need to make myself scarce for a few hours."

Prisha was the perfect friend. She didn't waste time asking questions, just fetched the van keys and led Landry and James through the storeroom to a back entrance.

"Go. Dinner and an explanation when you can. Take care, Landry." She gave him a brief hug.

"You might report a break-in at the antique store," James suggested

"Yes! But don't go over there. Wait for the cops," Landry said.

"I won't. Now go."

Landry didn't need to be told twice. He gave the van keys to James. "I'll probably crash if I drive. I don't get behind the wheel much."

"With the amount of stimulants in your system, I wouldn't let you behind the wheel of a tricycle."

"Hey!"

They ran across the yard to where the Emporium's van was parked.

"Get in, Landry."

The van smelled of oranges. There was a colorful model of the Lord Ganesha on the dashboard and a string of bright paper flowers hung from the rear-view mirror. Landry cranked a window.

"Where are we going?" he asked as James pulled out of the yard and into traffic.

"I know a place."

Landry slumped in his seat. "I've had enough adventures to last a lifetime."

"Ring Gage. Let him know what's going on."

"I left my phone in the store. Dammit!"

"Let's get clear of the area, then we can find a phone somewhere."

"I don't have my wallet either." Landry sighed. "I'm not very good at this."

James chuckled. "I think that's a good thing."

Landry lost track of the number of turns James made, but they ended up at a strip mall in SoDo, an area Landry didn't know well. James pulled into a vacant parking slot. There was a nail salon, a small grocery store, a drug store and a liquor store in the row. A storage facility squatted at one end while the other end boasted a Wendy's restaurant and drive-through. James pulled some bills from his wallet.

"Do you want to get some burgers, as we didn't get to eat the ones I bought earlier? I'm going to get some painkillers from the pharmacy. Then we should see if we can find a phone somewhere."

"Sure. Are you in a lot of pain?"

"Climbing down that fire escape ladder didn't do me any favors," James admitted.

Landry took the money then wandered over to Wendy's, glad for once that it wasn't raining. In escaping the store he'd left in just a T-shirt. *This kind of thing doesn't happen in the movies.* The irony of fetching take-out after escaping the Yakuza wasn't lost on him. By now, the police should be at the store and Gage would have been alerted. Landry decided food could wait until he'd called Gage. He backtracked to the drug store and went inside, but didn't spot James. He went to the counter. "I'm looking for my friend... Tall, blond and..."

"Gorgeous." The young redheaded assistant, whose nametag said Candy, grinned.

"That's him."

"He came in but said he'd forgotten his wallet. Then I think I spotted him walk past. He'll probably be back."

Confused, Landry went outside. *How could he have forgotten his wallet?* He wandered along the strip, peering in doors. He came face to face with James leaving the secure storage place. Landry gaped. "What exactly do you think you're doing?" He eyed the package in James' hands.

"Landry." James sounded exasperated. "Why couldn't you do what you were told for once?"

"Disobedience is a bad habit of mine. What do you have there?"

195

"What do you think?" James slipped the package into his inside jacket pocket.

"I doubt it's your secret baseball card collection."

"No, it isn't."

"You saw the number in my lucky cat, didn't you? You knew what it was."

"You did a good job at pretending not to be interested but I've been hunting the jewelry too, remember. It's my job."

"How did you know about this security box?"

James sighed. "Here and now isn't the time to be discussing this, Landry."

"So what are you going to do, ditch me and make a run for it?"

"You weren't supposed to see me picking this up. We were going to eat, call Gage, and then I would have arranged a meeting place to drop you off." He shook his head. "Now I'll have to change my plans somewhat."

"You can't make me come with you. Unless you have a gun. You don't, do you?"

"Of course not. Landry, you have no phone, no money, and you're wearing a thin T-shirt on a cold day. Unless you want to get hypothermic, I'd say your choices are limited and besides, I'm pretty sure I *can* make you come with me, even without a gun. I don't want to hurt you, well, not like this, anyway. But I need you to do as I say."

"You used me, you bastard. Were you even followed back to the store earlier?" A tear trickled down Landry's cheek and he brushed it away.

"No, though it was easy enough to convince you I was and yes, I'm afraid I did use you. I'm sorry about that. Genuinely. I like you a lot and under different circumstances I would have liked us to be friends, even if something more was never on the cards. You're very fortunate to have found a Dom like Gage." For a moment he seemed wistful. "We're going to walk back to the van now and you're not going to do anything stupid."

"Is your commission really worth this much to you?"

"If these jewels disappear into the warrens of Seattle PD, I'll never see them again. Once I return them to my insurance company, it'll become public that they've been found. I get paid and they get to deal with law enforcement. I have to hand them back in person or I don't see a penny."

"You're unbelievable." Landry considered his options but came to the conclusion that sticking with James for as long as possible was better than the alternatives. He didn't think James would hurt him unless he was cornered or desperate, and maybe, just maybe, Landry would find a way to get word to Gage.

* * * *

Sancha slammed her phone down, making her desk shake. "I'm gonna be old and gray before we track down this number." She scowled. "Don't say it."

"Say what?" Gage feigned innocence.

"Whatever it was you were about to say."

"You want more coffee?"

"That swill you keep bringing me could strip paint. No thanks, my stomach lining has had enough." She raked her hands through her hair. "Could this be any more frustrating? I've got everyone with a pulse working on this and some that don't and unless we get lucky, it'll take a week to get through all the calls."

Gage's phone rang. "Saved by the bell." He picked up, listened then grinned. "Yes!" He slammed the phone down almost as hard as Sancha. "Uniform just brought in Tadanobu Tsukamoto."

"Huh?"

"The lucky cat with the number written inside came from a crate of antiques delivered to Landry's store by his boss's nephew, Eddie Lao. Eddie got the crate from the grandson of a neighbor who had passed away. The grandson had ties to the Yakuza. Remember?"

"I'm not completely senile." Sancha pushed her chair back. "Why are you still sitting there?"

Gage shrugged at the sympathetic glances from several of his colleagues, most of who were terrified of Sancha. He got up. "Tadanobu Tsukamoto is known as The Ferret to his friends."

"Ferret?"

"What can I say? Who'd lie about that name? For simplicity, let's call him Tad."

Sancha marched across the squad room then down three flights of stairs to the floor that housed the interview rooms.

"Room four," Gage advised.

"He lawyered up yet?"

"Nope. Declined counsel. You want to take the lead on this one?"

Sancha twisted her lips into some semblance of a snarl. "Sure. Psycho girl cop usually gets 'em talking. He'll sing like he's in the confessional."

"I doubt he's Catholic. The main religions in Japan are Buddhism and Shintoism."

"Did you swallow Wikipedia? His only fucking religion is money if he's tied up with the Yakuza."

Gage didn't argue. Sancha was on a roll and he had no intention of stopping her.

"Well, that's not what I was expecting," Sancha said, staring through the one-way mirror into the interview room.

"Stop drooling," Gage admonished.

"Why? Look at him."

"It's unprofessional, and I am looking. How on earth did he get the nickname Ferret? I was expecting someone small and…ferrety." The young man pacing the interview room was gorgeous. Black hair cropped short, sharp cheekbones and lush lips. Even from a few meters away, Gage could see how green the man's eyes were. He was around six feet tall, slender, and several days' stubble covered a firm chin.

"I'd like to see him on a catwalk modeling swimwear," Sancha said. "And don't tell me you're not thinking the same thing."

"My thoughts are much, much less pure," Gage admitted.

"I'm telling Landry."

"I'm allowed to look — so long as I don't touch."

"He's straight. Gotta be."

Gage shook his head. "Nope. Definitely on my team."

"Five dollars."

"Done."

Sancha adjusted her expression from lustful to stern, then marched into the room. She slammed her notebook onto the table. "Take a seat. Mr. Tsukamoto."

"Tad is fine. Mr. Tsukamoto is my dad." Tad was pale. He sat, fingers tapping his knee in agitation.

"We've been looking for you, Tad. You're a hard man to find." Sancha sat opposite him. Gage remained standing.

"You wouldn't have found me at all if I hadn't wanted you to." Tad had a smooth, deep voice.

"You were stopped for speeding. The arresting officer saw the warrant for you in connection with the assault on an antique store assistant."

"I saw that motorbike cop from a quarter-mile away."

"So you're telling me you were deliberately speeding when you passed her?"

"Yes. I couldn't walk in here. I had to get arrested. I need help."

The interview wasn't going the way Gage had expected at all.

"And that's why you've waived counsel?"

"No lawyers, no recordings. I need protection—a safe place to stay."

"In return for…?"

"Enough information to put away the leaders of Seattle's biggest crime syndicate for a very long time."

"To be clear, you're talking about the Yakuza?"

"Yes."

"And you're looking for immunity from prosecution?"

"No. I'm a witness. I haven't done anything criminal."

Sancha's silence spoke volumes. Gage leaned against the wall, arms folded. "First things first. Tell us why Treasure Trove was targeted."

"That was my fault." Tad pinched the bridge of his nose. "I put an article in a box of antiques that ended up at the store—an item that had little value in itself but contained something of worth to some very dangerous people."

"The lucky cat," Gage said.

Tad nodded. "My grandmother died recently and my family had boxed up some stuff that was going to be sold. I put the cat in the crate when I was helping clear out her place. There was no way I could keep it anywhere it might be associated with me. I took the box over to a guy called Eddie Lao, who I knew by sight. He's the nephew of the guy that owns the antique store. He said he'd do me a favor and drop it off. I thought the cat would be safe in amongst the other antiques, but the Yakuza have spies everywhere. It didn't take them long to track down the crate."

"They knew about the cat?"

Tad shook his head. "No, not specifically. They knew I had the key. They turned my place over looking for it. I had a business card from Mr. Lao and they must've followed the trail."

"By sheer accident, the cat wasn't in the store when your friends paid a visit," Sancha said. "The shop assistant had a terrifying experience. He could have been killed."

"What do you mean, the cat wasn't there?"

"Because it was broken, the shop assistant had taken it to his apartment in the same building. He happened to collect lucky cats."

"Normal people collect baseball cards or matchbooks," Gage muttered.

"Is he okay?" Tad asked. "I really didn't mean for anyone to get hurt because of me."

"He's fine. So it was you who wrote the key code inside the cat?"

"Yes. I was given that cat as a kid. I broke it open, wrote the code inside then glued it back together. Did a pretty good job too, you could hardly see the break."

Gage moved to stand at the side of the table. "So where is the security box that the code unlocks? I assume it's a safety deposit box or something similar?"

"It's for a private storage facility. You know—one of those places that rents out small boxes, not one of the huge warehouses. It's called Guardian Storage, on Howell Way. They do an anonymous service. No names. No ID. You just need your box number and code."

"So the first two digits of the key are the box number and the last four the access code," Gage said. "What's in the box?"

"A package I was asked to store for a friend."

"What friend?" Gage snapped.

"You don't need to know that.

"I'd guess that package contains some very valuable jewelry," Sancha said. "From a heist in Japan a while back. We've already recovered some of the other stolen property. The question is, why was the jewelry separate from the rest of the stuff and why was it sent to you?"

Tad shrugged. "I'm not telling you anything else until I know I'm getting protection."

Sancha grunted. "You get to stay here while we check out the storage place. If what you say is true and we find the package, then we'll talk." She shoved her chair back then she left the room, Gage close behind her.

"What do you think?" Sancha asked once they had briefed the duty officer to keep Tad under lock and key until they returned.

"I think he's telling the truth," Gage said. "He's scared, despite the bravado. Perhaps one of the crew that carried out the raid in Japan betrayed the plan and took the jewels."

"How did they get them across the Pacific?"

Gage shrugged. "I wouldn't be surprised if they were put in the mail. A small package. Not everything gets checked."

"You think it could be that simple?" Sancha asked.

"Why not? The simplest plans are sometimes the most successful. Let's go, we'll take the Jeep."

The drive across town to Guardian Storage took around twenty minutes. Gage found a parking spot right outside.

"Talk about hiding in plain sight," Sancha said. "It would have taken us weeks to track down this place. We were checking the more obvious ones first. Whoever's behind this would have known that."

"Clever." Gage had a grudging respect for whoever had masterminded the theft. He led the way into the front office where a receptionist staffed a single desk. She looked bored. Gage flashed his badge. "Where are the storage boxes?"

"In the back." She made no attempt to ask for a warrant. Gage went to the door she indicated. Inside, there had to be five hundred boxes. It didn't take long for Gage to find box thirty-two.

He punched in the key code then pulled open the door. "Fuck." There was nothing inside except a single piece of paper. "Someone beat us to it," he said, handing the paper to Sancha.

"*Too late.*" Sancha read from the sheet. "Cocky bastard."

Gage banged the side of the metal cabinetry. "We should get the crime scene people out here but I'd bet good money they won't find anything."

"Let's go see if Alison can tell us anything?"

"Alison?" Gage was confused.

"The receptionist. One of us bothered to ask the poor woman her name." Sancha rolled her eyes. "Call yourself a detective."

Gage opened his mouth to respond but couldn't think of anything suitable to say so he closed it again and walked past Sancha into the front office, ignoring her gleeful cackle. He approached the assistant, who was deep in conversation on her desk phone.

"Alison, I'd like to ask you a few questions," Gage said.

"Sure," she said. "Gotta go, sweetie." She ended her call.

"Has anyone else been in today to access the boxes?"

"Yup, not so long ago in fact. One guy came in, got something out of a box. He met someone else outside. I could see them through the door. They walked off together."

"Can you describe them?"

"The first guy was tall, blond, very good looking. I noticed him because I prefer blonds. She shrugged. "I'd have to have been dead *not* to notice him. He looked like a movie star or something."

"And the other guy," Gage prompted.

"He was cute too. Smaller, about my height. Blond as well, but a lighter shade. He was just wearing a T-shirt and pants, which seemed strange because it's quite cold out."

"Do you have any CCTV?" Sancha asked.

"We do," Alison said. "But the cameras weren't working today. Some kind of electrical fault."

"Thank you. Don't let anyone into that room. We'll be sending someone over to dust for prints. The cops will also take a formal statement from you."

"Were those guys criminals?" Alison asked, her face reddening.

"I'm afraid I can't talk about an ongoing investigation, ma'am," Gage said. "But thank you for your cooperation."

He and Sancha headed outside. "I don't know what's going on, partner, but those two could only be James Ellery and Landry." He pulled out his phone and sent a text to Landry asking him to call back. "I think we should drive over to Treasure Trove."

Sancha's phone rang and she hauled it out of her purse. She listened to the call, frowned then tossed the phone back in her purse. "We need to get over there right now. Someone's reported a break-in. Operations just let me know because we put that alert on any incidents in the area of the store."

Gage stared at his cell, willing it to ring. He called Landry's number but it went to voicemail. "Where the hell is he?"

"Stop talking, start driving," Sancha said. "The sooner we get there, the sooner you'll find out."

Chapter Sixteen

"I can't believe you went to a drive-through," Landry said, clutching the bag of burgers and fries that James had thrust at him.

"I'm hungry and I imagine you are too...because you always are."

Landry's stomach chose that moment to rumble. "Oh, for fuck's sake." Landry stuck his hand in the bag. He pulled out a burger, unwrapped it then took a huge bite. "Oh, that's so good."

"Extra cheese. Are you going to give me one, or is this your way of punishing me?" James asked.

"Find somewhere to pull over. I'm not going to become an accident statistic because you were eating and driving." Landry didn't feel like being cooperative. He kept munching, making lots of appreciative noises. It was a small revenge but so worth it. James pulled into the lot of a Walgreens, taking a spot near the back, away from the store.

"Give me the food, Landry, or I swear I will spank you right here."

Landry was about to say there wasn't enough room but the back of the van had ample space. He thrust a burger at James. "Choke on it, you're not getting anywhere near my ass."

James ate the burger in a few swift bites. "Junk food is always best in a crisis, I find."

"This is a crisis?"

"You want me to tell you how I knew about the secure box?"

Landry nodded.

"Then be nice."

"Fine, but this is a temporary suspension of hostilities." Landry shoved a handful of fries into his mouth.

"I'll bet Gage uses a gag on you."

Landry glared but ate more fries. "You'll never know."

"I robbed the robbers."

"Huh?" It was difficult to express a lack of understanding with his mouth full. Landry chewed, swallowed then took a breath. "I don't understand."

"It's not that difficult, Landry. I stole the jewels from the people that stole them in the first place. I needed to get rid of them as quickly as possible so I mailed them to a friend with instructions to store the package at the Guardian Storage place."

"You airmailed priceless jewels?"

"Why not?"

"I… Unbelievable. Why Guardian?"

"Obscure. Plenty of people around. Safe enough to slip in there without being observed and they have an anonymous service. I found it online."

"But you didn't have the box number or code."

"No. I was traveling. I didn't want my friend to risk making unnecessary contact. We were supposed to meet once I got to Seattle, but by the time I got here he was in trouble and had gone to ground. I had to be careful. Somehow, someone identified me in Japan. I had the Yakuza after me on both sides of the Pacific. I decided my best bet was to attach myself to the detective investigating the case over here and that led me to you."

"How did you know the lucky cat had ended up at the store?"

"I didn't. You were my route to Gage. I hoped he would talk about the case to you then I'd persuade you to talk to me but then the Yakuza attacked you at the store and I knew there had to be something I was missing."

"You were watching me."

"Fortunate for you that I was."

"So how did you get beaten up?"

"I heard a rumor on the grapevine that some of the stolen goods that had reached the States were about to be moved to a private collector. When you've been in the investigation business as long as I have…well, I have a network of informants. I got a bit too close."

"You tipped off the cops, didn't you?"

"Yes."

"What about the piece of paper Gage's partner found at the raid?"

"Me again, I'm afraid. Hints to the right people, a scribbled note shoved in a mailbox. I was trying to put them off the scent. Unfortunately it backfired."

"You manipulative, lying son of a bitch," Landry snapped. "I could have been killed but I don't suppose you care. You've gotten what you wanted." Landry thought he detected a hint of color on James' cheeks but his expression revealed nothing.

"I didn't count on liking you." James turned on the ignition. "Time to drop you off. It should be safe to go back to Treasure Trove by now."

"And by safe you mean...for you, not me."

"Less cops. Relaxed vigilance. They won't find any trace of Yakuza, after all."

"The people I saw. The shadows outside the window...."

"Could have been anyone. Handy timing that they showed up when they did."

"I hope Prisha doesn't get into trouble for calling in a false alarm."

"She'll tell the cops about us getting away, won't she? She'll be fine."

Landry sulked on the drive back. He wanted to shout and scream but instead seethed and muttered. He did notice how tightly James gripped the steering wheel, his knuckles bleached with tension.

Good. He should be stressed after what he's put me through. Why didn't I see him for what he was? I'm such a fucking idiot. Gage was right not to trust him. Idiot. Idiot. Idiot.

Three blocks from the store, James pulled over. "I think you can make it the rest of the way on your own."

"You're leaving?"

"Did you expect me to drive right up to your boyfriend and let him arrest me?"

"I... That would be nice."

"I'm not nice."

"No fucking kidding."

"It was fun knowing you, Landry." James got out of the van. "I'll be seeing you."

"Not if I see you first," Landry snapped, even though he knew it made no sense. He shifted into the driver's seat then watched in the rear-view mirror while James crossed the street, hailed a cab and was gone.

With a heavy sigh, Landry drove up the street, thankful that it wasn't far. Gage's Jeep and two cop cars were parked outside the store. Landry swerved into a space on the opposite side of the street, in front of the Eastern Emporium. He bumped the curb and wasn't anywhere close to aligned but he didn't care. Prisha came running out. Landry had barely got out of the van before she was crushing him in a monster hug.

"What have you got yourself into, Landry? I rang the cops like your friend said. Where is he by the way? He was cute. Is he single? And anyway, they were here so fast! There were people swarming all over the store, I think they broke your door again…it was like the Wild West! I don't know if they found any bad guys. Life hasn't been so exciting round here since that dumpster fire two years ago. My dad says you're a bad influence but he still sent me out here to check on you. How's the van? You didn't kill it, did you? And, by the way, you can't park worth a damn. How did you ever get your license?"

Landry extricated himself from Prisha's arms. "Honey, we'll have to catch up another time. I have to go let the cops know I'm back and still have all my limbs. The van is unharmed but I owe you some gas money."

Prisha waved him away. "How many favors have you done me? Forget it. Call me when you can."

"I will." Landry jogged across the street to the store. He could see that the door had been forced, though not smashed in like the last time. Landry explained who he was to the cop standing guard then got ushered inside. Sancha spotted him before Gage. She gave Gage a sharp elbow in the ribs.

"Look who just came in."

"Landry." Landry didn't have a chance to get closer. Gage flew toward him, scooping him off the floor into a tight embrace. After putting him down, Gage gave Landry a thorough examination. "You're okay."

"I think you just crushed a few ribs, but yes. My pride is a bit battered but the rest of me is intact."

"Where's that fucking Brit? He was supposed to be taking care of you."

"Gone. I have so much to tell you. You're not gonna believe it." Landry discovered his legs were shaking. "I think I need to sit down." He hung on to Gage's arm.

"Can you make it upstairs? You can tell Sancha and me everything over a cup of tea."

"Tea! You're joking, right?"

"Isn't everyone supposed to drink tea in an emergency?" Gage attempted to hide a smile.

"Stop teasing me! I've had a very bad day." Landry gave Gage's arm a half-hearted slap. He surveyed the store but, apart from the broken door, couldn't see much damage.

"There's no sign that anyone got into the store before the locals arrived. We've checked the storeroom and the cash register. There's cash still in it."

"There wasn't anyone here. It was all a ploy to get me away from the store. I didn't know that when James told Prisha to call the cops." A wave of fatigue washed over Landry. "If Mr. Lao doesn't fire me, he'll have me doing inventory every night for the rest of my life."

Sancha patted his shoulder. "He'll understand. None of this is your fault, Landry. Blind chance and coincidence got us to this point."

Landry retrieved his phone from beneath the counter. "I left this in the panic to get out. Oh, there's a text from Mr. Lao—he says the grandson's name is Tadanobu Tsukamoto."

"We know. We have him in custody," Sancha said.

"Too little, too late. Seems I'm always three steps behind everyone else," Landry said. "I would have liked to be the gay Miss Marple."

"Not Hercule Poirot?" Sancha asked.

"With that mustache?" He led the way upstairs to his apartment where he grabbed a glass and a bottle of wine from the fridge. Sancha and Gage were on duty so they declined his offer to share. Landry had no capacity for alcohol, but it seemed like the right time to drown his sorrows a little. He needed something to get him through the retelling of his day to Sancha and Gage and it was easier to hide behind a glass, not wanting to see their expressions, whether they be of pity or sympathy. Or worse, in Gage's case, disappointment. Landry felt like an idiot. Despite everything, there had been something about James Ellery that had appealed to him. Not in the same way that Gage appealed, because Gage pushed every button Landry possessed, but James Ellery had a hint of mystery about him and Landry had been intrigued. He was also a sucker for anything hurt or injured, and there was no way he would have been able to throw Ellery out on the street the previous night. It just wasn't in his nature to be so callous and it had seemed to him that he and James shared a common enemy.

He sat at his small dining table, Gage on one side, Sancha on the other, and recounted the events of the day as best he was able. When he got to the part at the drive-through, Sancha snorted with laughter.

"That man sure has brass balls," she crowed. "I'm almost sorry I couldn't get to know him."

Landry glared at her. Then the humor of the situation broke through his embarrassment and he smiled. "It was a bit surreal. The fries were good, though."

Gage reached for Landry's hand and gave his fingers a squeeze. "He was very convincing, you know."

"You didn't trust him." Landry grabbed Gage's hand, holding on tight.

"He doesn't trust anyone," Sancha said. "Neither of us do. It goes with the job. Keep your innocence, Landry, it suits you."

"Is it innocence, or naïveté? I think I'd rather be streetwise."

"That wouldn't suit you," Gage said. "You handled the situation today really well. You were brave. Getting out of here, thinking of the van... And from the sound of it, James never had any intention of you finding out about the jewels. It was his bad luck that you found him out."

Landry took another two big swallows of wine. "Has he actually committed a crime? I mean, he stole the jewels from people who had already stolen them. He claimed his intention was always to give them back."

"A prosecution would be difficult," Gage admitted. "Theoretically, he acted in the best interests of his clients, and in his own, of course. But he should have told the authorities about what was going on, rather than try to handle it himself. He put a lot of people in danger through his actions."

"What about the grandson?" Landry asked. "What will happen to him now?"

"It wouldn't surprise me at all," Gage said, "if it was James Ellery who advised Tad to seek help from us. I'd guess they have some kind of relationship. I can't see why Tad would have helped him hide the jewels otherwise, and I don't see him being motivated solely by money. He risked his life betraying the Yakuza and he has a lot more information outside of the jewel theft. I would imagine he'll be offered protective custody and then witness protection."

"That's kind of sad," Landry said. "If he and James are together, even if James is a snake, that'll be it for them, won't it?"

"Even James Ellery would have a hard time tracking Tad down in witness protection," Sancha said. Landry and Gage exchanged a knowing look. "Though anything is possible, I suppose."

Landry giggled. His glass was empty. He went to pour himself another, but Gage took the bottle away.

"That's enough for you, young man." Landry pouted. "Don't give me that look," Gage said.

"You're not the boss of me." Landry touched the chain around his neck. "Okay, you are but..."

"Do you want a monster headache when you have to work tomorrow?"

"S'pose not," Landry admitted. "But at the moment it seems like a good idea to get completely, utterly drunk."

Sancha's phone rang. She got up then moved away to answer it.

"If you're drunk, we won't be able to play tonight," Gage said, keeping his voice low.

Landry narrowed his eyes. "That's bribery."

"Is it working?"

"Depends. What are you going to do to me?"

"Tie you up then fuck you. A lot."

"I'll make myself a coffee." Landry got up to go to the kitchen.

"Hold on a bit, Landry." Sancha returned. "The patrolman at the front door of the shop called to say he has a package for you."

"For me?" Landry realized it was a dumb question as soon as he said it.

"Yep. Hand delivered."

"That sounds kind of suspicious in the circumstances, doesn't it?" Landry turned to Gage, hoping he didn't come across as paranoid.

"It does." Gage frowned. "The uniform describe who handed it over?"

"A teenage kid. He kept hold of him," Sancha said.

"Then we'd best go take a look." Gage got up. "Not you, Landry."

"Hey! It's my package. I'm not staying here all alone while the two of you get to do all the fun stuff. And don't tell me to do as I'm told."

"Stubborn, isn't he?" Sancha grinned.

"He's a brat." Gage sighed. "Fine. But I open the parcel, not you."

"Why, you don't think it'll explode do you? Or be full of snakes?" Landry gulped. "You don't...do you?"

"No, I don't but it's better I open it, just in case."

"So it's okay for you to be hurt but not me?"

"That's the way it works."

"There's no point arguing with him, Landry," Sancha said. "There are rocks in Yosemite less immoveable than him."

"I'm beginning to realize that," Landry muttered. "Stubborn, overprotective..." He caught Gage's eye. "All right!"

"I suspect you won't be sitting comfortably tomorrow, sweetie," Sancha whispered in Landry's ear.

Landry gaped. He had no idea Sancha know about Gage's proclivities for BDSM.

"No secrets between partners." She bumped hips with him. "And the chain is a bit of a giveaway, you know. That's his St. Christopher, and I know what you wearing it means."

Landry touched the pendant. "I suppose it is."

"He's never given one of those to anyone else. Gage takes care of everyone, often at his own expense. He's gonna be uber-possessive about you, so you might as well get used to it. He'd never forgive himself if anything happened to you when he could have prevented it."

"If you two have quite finished whispering about me," Gage said. "Shall we go?"

They trooped back down to the store. Gage, who had fetched the mysterious parcel from his colleague out on the street, laid it on the cash desk. The outer wrapping was plain brown paper and Landry's name was scrawled on the top. Gage removed the outer layer, wearing a pair of latex gloves. He handed the paper to a crime scene tech who was hovering nearby. "I'll doubt you'll find anything on it, but you should check it anyway," he said. "You'll need to get elimination prints from the teenager who delivered it."

"What is it?" Sancha asked.

"A Japanese puzzle box," Landry said, admiring the detailed marquetry of the wooden object before him.

"You're gonna have to enlighten me," Sancha said.

"They are really clever craftsmen-produced boxes, which take several steps to open, usually involving hidden, sliding panels, drawers, buttons... That kind of thing. Some are very simple and only have one or two steps, others have many more. Often, they don't have instructions and you have to work out the secrets for yourself. This is quite a big one. We've had older ones in the store on occasion, but nothing this beautiful. It's a work of art."

"There's a note," Gage said. He pulled a slip of paper from beneath the box, holding it up so that Landry could read it without touching it.

"We know what we are, but know not what we may be." Landry grabbed his phone. "I think that's Shakespeare. Let me check."

"It's that fucking Brit, isn't it?" Gage said, scowling.

"It's from *Hamlet*," Landry said. "Ophelia says it, but I doubt that's relevant."

"Cryptic. Why can't people speak plain English?" Gage handed the box to the tech. "Can you give this a quick dusting?" She took it away and a few minutes later returned.

"It's been wiped clean. No marks at all, not even a partial."

Gage handed the box to Landry. "Do you think you can open it?"

"I can have a go."

In the end it took Landry almost an hour to decipher the various levels of the puzzle box. Gage stayed with him the whole time, while Sancha went out to fetch coffee. She returned with three large cups and a box of donuts.

"Brain food."

"I've done it," Landry said, sliding the last section away to reveal the inner cavity. "There's something in here." He pulled out a black velvet pouch. It had some weight and something inside clinked when Landry jiggled it. He opened the pouch, upended it then shook the contents into Gage's palm. "Holy crap."

Flashes of light shone from the facets of multiple diamonds set into a heavy gold necklace. Landry did a quick count. "There are over fifty diamonds in this."

"Fifty-two, they add up to a total weight of over a hundred carats," Gage said. "It's worth around eight million dollars."

"It's the piece that was stolen from the Tokyo exhibition," Sancha said. "It's a lot more beautiful in real life than in the pictures we've seen."

"But why has James Ellery given it up?" Landry wondered, staring at the gems. "He doesn't have a conscience, so it can't be guilt."

"An apology of sorts?" Gage suggested. "Is there anything else in the bag?"

"Another note. This one isn't quite so cryptic," Landry said, handing it to Gage.

"So the man does have a heart after all," Gage said. *"Tell your detective to take care of Tad.* I knew those two had to be in some kind of relationship. You owe me five dollars, partner."

"It's kind of romantic," Landry said.

"It's one hell of a gesture," Sancha added. "He'll lose his commission for handing this over to us. The necklace will be held up in the evidence chain for months." She gave Gage a five.

"I don't understand," Landry said. "He retrieved it—why wouldn't he get paid?"

"The only way he can prove he found it is for him to hand it over in person." Gage slipped the necklace back into the pouch. "Even if he was only on a five percent commission, he's just given up four hundred thousand dollars, and I'd guess he was on a higher rate than that."

"Wow." Landry didn't know what to say. He picked out a chocolate custard donut from the box Sancha had brought and took a huge bite.

"I still don't like him," Gage muttered.

Sancha and Landry shared a look then both dissolved into hysterics.

Chapter Seventeen

"Four weeks. It's been four weeks. A whole month and I'm still not used to how stupid early you get up," Landry complained.

"Sometimes there are advantages to getting up early," Gage said, admiring the scene he had created. Landry, naked and fresh from the shower, was bent over the back of the couch, hands cuffed behind his back. His nipples were clamped and he was blindfolded. "You make the sweetest little whimpering noises." Gage pressed close behind Landry, letting him know how hard Gage was. He reached around Landry's body to flick the clamps. Landry moaned and shuddered. "I think I could make you come doing that."

"Hurts so good." Landry stuck his ass out. "Need you, Sir."

Gage stroked Landry's flanks then let his hands roam to Landry's flat belly and hair-free groin. "So smooth." Gage gripped Landry's cock at the same moment he pushed into his body.

"Oh!"

"Good boy. I've got you." Since they'd gotten tested, Gage had never tired of the novelty of having latex-free contact between him and Landry. "Made for me." He moved slowly, the long smooth strokes building to something wilder and less controlled. Landry's fingers curled into fists and he tugged at his bonds.

"Harder...please, Sir!"

Gage slowed even more and Landry sobbed.

"Who's in charge, Landry?"

"You are, Sir!"

"That's right, and what does that mean?"

"You decide how fast...you say how..." Landry's voice hitched.

"I decide if you get to come." Gage squeezed Landry's rigid shaft. "It's been too long since you spent some time in a cage. Since I have to work today, it's the perfect opportunity to try the new one I bought for you." At the thought of Landry locked in chastity, Gage could no longer contain himself. He pounded Landry's ass so hard the couch moved several inches. Landry's pleas for more reassured Gage that he wasn't being too rough. He obliged, driving as deep as he could while fisting Landry's cock. There wasn't much rhythm or coordination involved but it had the desired effect. Landry came in hot spurts that coated Gage's hand and a few seconds later, as if triggered by the scent of Landry's release, Gage pumped his seed into Landry's channel. "Fuck..." He thrust again, his orgasm continuing unabated. Limp, Landry sagged over the furniture, moaning. Gage pulled him upright and, once he'd slipped free of Landry's body, turned him around for a sticky, messy hug and a demanding kiss. Landry leaned against him, humming his pleasure.

"We need another shower," Gage said.

"'kay. And coffee. And waffles. Why do you have to work on a Sunday again?"

"I told you—Sancha and I are on rotation. If I had any choice I'd be here with you, you know that." Gage walked Landry to the bathroom, managing not to knock into anything on the way. He washed his hands before removing Landry's blindfold and cuffs. Landry gazed up at him.

"You're all flushed."

"Big shock. So are you. Clamps next."

Landry pouted. "No fair." Gage removed both clamps in tandem and Landry shrieked. "Oh, oh, oh...ow! Why does it hurt so much more when they come off than when they go on?" He rubbed at his chest.

"This set is quite tame. I have a pair that are much harsher than these."

"I don't think I want to meet those if it's all the same to you, Sir."

"We'll see." Gage squeezed into Landry's shower alongside him. It wasn't big enough for much fun but Gage enjoyed soaping Landry's smooth skin and teasing him. He spent some quality time playing with Landry's swollen nipples, making him squeal. Once they were done and Landry was dry, Gage fetched his new acquisition from the bedroom.

"What the ever-loving heck is that?" Landry eyed the device.

"Isn't it great? It's called a tailpipe chastity cock-lock." Gage held out the black device. "It's very flexible. Your cock goes in the tube, the bar sits nice and snug between your legs and the plug, once it's in your ass, holds the chastity tube in place. Genius."

Landry prodded the silicone. "Who thinks up the names for these things? Ooh, it's squishy!"

"It's designed to be worn for a long time." Gage fitted the tube section over Landry's flaccid cock before lubing the plug. He pushed the bulbous section into Landry's well-stretched ass. "Perfect."

"How long is long?"

"As long as I say."

"It doesn't have a lock," Landry said, squirming.

"No, it doesn't. I trust you not to take it off."

Landry's eyes grew big and round.

"What do you have planned for the day?"

"I... How do you expect me to concentrate? This thing is big. It's pushing on my fun button and my dick is screaming at me because it can't do what comes naturally."

"You call your prostate your fun button?" Gage rubbed at his hair with a towel.

"Why not? Prostate is so...clinical."

"I've known you a month and it's the first time you've used it."

"I'm full of surprises." Landry waddled to the bedroom. "Oh God, this feels weird. The joining piece is rubbing between my legs...it's...frustrating!"

"Good." Gage dressed. There would be time to make waffles before he had to leave to meet Sancha and he knew Landry had some blueberries stashed in the fridge. "So...your plans?"

"I'm gonna sit and throw darts at your picture, or maybe sew one of those voodoo doll thingies so I can stick pins in you."

"Uh huh." Gage headed for the kitchen.

"It's only fair I should get to torture you too."

Gage smiled, gathering what he needed to make waffle batter. "I can fit in time during my day to think up new punishments for you, you know?"

Landry glared. "Fine. Mr. Lao is back tomorrow so I'm going to get some groceries for him and give his apartment a clean. Once that's done, I intend to spend the entire afternoon on the couch, watching anime and eating snacks. I can't believe Mr. Lao extended his trip. He owes me some major vacation time."

"The last few weeks haven't been so bad though, have they?"

"No, much better since I stopped trying to manage on my own." Once his friends had learned of Landry's adventures, they had rallied round to help in the store. Prisha had covered for him at lunchtimes so that he could go out to eat, sometimes meeting up with Gage and Sancha at their favorite diner. It worked much better than trying to find a good time to close for an hour. His friend Petey from Scorch had come along to keep him company once he'd finished work and even Basim had shown up with treats and helped out with a few customers when the store got busy. The neighborhood had a strong community spirit and Landry had learned a new appreciation for people's willingness to help out. He had done as Mr. Lao suggested and closed the store an hour earlier each night, which meant that he felt rested during the day. He had also Skyped with Mr. Lao, Gage sitting alongside him, so that he could explain what had been going on rather than keep worrying about what he was going to say. Mr. Lao had shown nothing but concern for Landry's health and safety, berating him for not nagging him about fitting an alarm system, which he promised to do as soon as he got back. Gage had offered to put him in touch with someone who did regular work for the police and Mr. Lao had accepted. Gage and Mr. Lao had gotten on remarkably well, chatting away about Landry's bad habits, his coffee addiction and the amount of sugar he consumed. Strangely, it wasn't annoying but comforting.

"Accepting help is a good thing. From what I've heard, you've done people a lot of favors in the past. They're all more than happy to help you out." Gage cooked and they ate far too many waffles with whipped cream and blueberries. Landry sucked down two mugs of coffee.

"It's good to have friends. How about you? Anything exciting lined up?"

"The paperwork on the Yakuza case is killing us. We're prepping for a few more arrests thanks to information from Tad. For once, the other alphabets seem grateful for our help. Probably because we're doing all the leg-work."

"This whole thing turned into a really big deal, didn't it?"

"An international deal. There have been arrests in Japan, Hong Kong and London as well as here in the US."

"Any trace of James Ellery?"

"Not so far, but I have some feelers out. We'll find him sooner or later and I'll sleep better once I know where he's lurking." Gage checked his watch. "I have to go. You okay to clear up?"

"Sure. Give Sancha a hug from me."

Gage kissed Landry, wishing that he didn't have to leave him. "I'll be home as early as I can. Pick out a paddle for later." Thinking about the prospect of

Landry over his knees, bare ass glowing, would get Gage through the day. Landry beamed.

"I'll be waiting."

"On your knees. Naked."

Landry blushed, the pink spreading to his collarbone. Gage fixed the image in his mind before heading out to work.

* * * *

"The diamonds are fake," Gage stated, looking at his partner across the table at Pops' diner where they were sharing an enormous bowl of nachos.

"The necklace?" Sancha asked. "What do you mean it's fake?"

"Not real," Gage confirmed. "It's a very, very good copy of the original."

"So let me get this straight," Sancha said, before stuffing a cheese-coated nacho in her mouth. She crunched for a few seconds, looking thoughtful. "The Yakuza stole a necklace from an exhibition in Tokyo, but the necklace was fake. James Ellery then stole a fake necklace from the Yakuza but, after significant shenanigans, gave it back."

"That's about it," Gage said. "I had a call about it earlier this morning. I thought it best to let you know when you weren't hungry." *Because you have a tendency to get feral when you haven't eaten.*

"Good decision on your part," Sancha said. "You have that look on your face. There's more, isn't there?"

"This is just speculation on my part, but what if the necklace that the Yakuza stole from the exhibition had already been stolen?"

"I haven't eaten enough nachos for this level of confusion," Sancha complained. "Explain it again and pretend like I'm a three-year-old."

Gage rolled his eyes. "I suspect that James Ellery is not quite what he seems. Oh, his cover is genuine enough. He *is* a registered investigator. He does work for major insurance companies. But I think he's also a thief."

Sancha shoveled more nachos into her mouth, licking up a stray drop of sour cream. "I'm gonna need popcorn too."

"I think Ellery stole the original necklace then replaced it with a fake. I think the original robbery had been planned for a very long time. It was incredible bad luck that the Yakuza targeted the exhibition and stole the replacement necklace, because if the exhibition had gone ahead as planned, it's unlikely that the fake would ever have been discovered. Or at least, not for many months, if not years."

"So, you think he's like some international man of mystery cat burglar or something?"

"I did a bit of research on our Mr. Ellery," Gage said. "With the help of some friends from Scotland Yard and contacts at Interpol. He has a very interesting travel record. He goes abroad a lot, which is perfectly legitimate with his work, but over the last ten years, Mr. Ellery has been in several countries where major jewel thefts have occurred, only he has been there up to two months before the thefts. He appears again once the robberies have occurred, because he's ostensibly investigating the cases."

"So, you think that he's replacing expensive jewelry with fakes when he steals them, only to go through the motions of recovering them for insurance companies further down the line. Even though what he's recovering are fakes."

"Yes." Gage drummed his fingers on the table. "He doesn't do it often. Most of his insurance recoveries are genuine. Let's face it, with historical heirlooms, lots of families in difficulties had to sell expensive pieces in the past and to save face, replaced them with copies. Who's to say how long the jewels have been fake. In most cases, there would be no way of proving when they had been replaced or even if it had been done in a criminal way. Generations could have passed since the originals were swapped over and unless new valuations by an expert had taken place, no one would ever know."

"It does kind of explain why he was prepared to mail eight million dollars' worth of necklace across an ocean." Sancha frowned. "That always seemed high risk to me. I don't even get my mail order deliveries from Amazon sometimes, and don't even ask me about DHL." She waved Pops over. "Pops, can we get two chocolate milkshakes with whipped cream, sprinkles and anything else you want to throw in there? We need them."

"Right away." Pops wandered off, smiling.

"I need sugar in the worst way," Sancha said.

"I can sympathize. I think Ellery will have already sold the real jewels. He could have broken the necklace up, sold the stones individually or as a collection, melted down the setting. If he's as ruthless as I suspect, he would have no qualms about destroying a historic piece."

"Are we ever going to be able to prove it, though?"

"I doubt it. I have to have grudging respect for the man. He must have nerves of steel."

"Are you going to tell Landry?"

"Why not?" Gage said. "It's all just a theory, after all. It will be down to the insurance company to deal with the fallout from discovering the jewels are fake, and everything else that was taken from the exhibition robbery has been recovered now. I suppose they'll have to authenticate everything, though I'm convinced Ellery is only interested in jewels. Tad gave us enough information to put away several influential leaders of the Yakuza. We'll be clearing up old cases for years because of his evidence. Everyone in the authorities on this side of the pond is quite content with the outcome. Why would they care one way or the other whether the jewels were swapped at some point in the past? More trouble than it's worth to head down that rabbit hole."

"This conversation is giving me heartburn," Sancha said. "What brought on this spate of philosophizing?"

"I was going through the paperwork this morning and found a reference to the quote that was included in the package with the Japanese puzzle box sent to Landry," Gage said. "It implied that there was more to James Ellery than met the eye. I think he's arrogant enough to drop that kind of hint."

"The quote was from Ophelia, right? Wasn't she driven mad by the men in her life?"

"Did you just betray a secret interest in literature or are you suggesting I drive you mad?"

"One of the kids is reading *Hamlet* at school."

"Right."

Pops arrived with the milkshakes. Sancha guzzled half of hers in one go. "Perhaps Ellery will show up again, one day."

"It wouldn't surprise me in the least," Gage said. "But I'll be on the lookout. I don't want him getting close to Landry ever again. He brings trouble with him."

"And Landry is enough of a handful as it is," Sancha said, laughing.

"You've got that right."

"Ah, look how the big bad detective is smitten."

Gage shrugged. "Can't disagree." He shifted his milkshake closer before Sancha could steal it and drink it too. "I'll make some notes, pass them over to Interpol and Scotland Yard. Maybe someone somewhere will take a closer look at Mr. James Ellery."

"Or maybe he'll track down his boyfriend in witness protection and live happily ever after."

"With the value of that necklace, that could have been his plan all along. To retire, settle down. If he has genuinely found somebody to put up with his arrogant ass, it could be possible," Gage said. "Witness protection wouldn't be much of a barrier to him, I'm sure."

"It would be nice to think that everyone gets their happy ever after."

"He's a bad guy, Sancha. A criminal. You aren't supposed to be empathizing with him."

Sancha shrugged. "Everyone deserves to find love."

"I promise not to tell anyone what a hopeless romantic you are underneath that feisty exterior," Gage said.

"No one would believe you anyway." Sancha grabbed what was left of his milkshake, her expression daring him to protest. Then she slurped it down with a satisfied grin.

Chapter Eighteen

Landry surveyed the store with a deep sense of satisfaction. He had dusted, polished and swept the place to within an inch of its life. Everything gleamed and the smell of beeswax permeated the air. It had been a great week for sales and Mr. Lao had been so pleased he had promised Landry a few days off. He and Gage were planning a road trip to the Grand Canyon in Gage's sister's camper. They also had an invitation to dinner with Landry's extended family, which Landry had been putting off. After three months of invitations, his mother had threatened to come to the store and drag him out by the hair if he didn't bring Gage over. *Still, Gage can handle anyone, even my evil twin brothers. They'll probably end up playing football in the backyard or something.* Landry would be quite happy spectating and gossiping with his mum.

He went through the routine of locking up, humming to himself. On his return from Hong Kong, Mr. Lao had not only installed a state-of-the-art alarm, but intercoms with video screens in both apartments so

Landry no longer had to run to the street gate to meet any evening visitors. The last few weeks had been busy and he and Gage had had little time for dating but tonight they were heading to Scorch. Landry couldn't wait to get dressed up and show Gage off to all his friends. He trotted up the stairs to his apartment, sneezing on the first-floor landing as usual. He'd only been to Gage's place a few times. It was a rental and didn't have much of a homely feel, though it was far bigger than Landry's apartment. Landry thought that his place was cozier. Gage seemed to have no objection to spending most nights in Landry's bed and besides, it was much easier for Landry not to have to travel into the store in the mornings. Gage had been moving more and more things into Landry's closet and bathroom and Landry found he loved discovering Gage's clothes in the laundry hamper, or remnants of his stubble on the edge of the sink.

Landry took a shower then prepped with care, not knowing what Gage might have in mind for the evening. He wanted to get dressed, but Gage had given him instructions that meant waiting a while. After throwing together a light meal of chicken salad, which he washed down with a glass of mineral water, he idled away the time playing Candy Crush on his phone. Gage was due at nine and, for once, was prompt. Landry heard his key in the lock at ten to the hour. He shrugged out of the robe he had been wearing then dropped to his knees just inside the door, head bowed.

"Well, that's the kind of sight I like to see after a long day at work," Gage said once he was inside. He ruffled Landry's hair.

"I hope you had a good day, Sir."

"It was interesting." Gage took Landry's hand, pulling him to his feet. He tilted his chin then kissed him, long and slow. His hands roamed, touching Landry's bare skin, stroking all Landry's most sensitive parts. Landry shivered, but tried to hold still while Gage explored.

"Shall we go to the bedroom?" Gage said. "I need to change and you need to put something on."

"I'm glad you don't want me to go to Scorch like this," Landry said.

"It has possibilities." Gage gave him a wicked grin. The clientele at Scorch weren't known for being shy and retiring. There would almost certainly be some subs there wearing little or nothing.

Landry skipped to his bedroom where he had laid out his clothes for the night. It had been months since he'd had the chance to wear his rubber gear and he couldn't wait to feel the slick constriction of latex against his skin.

"Before you dress," Gage said, "I have a few accessories for you." He dumped his overnight bag on the bed then pulled out a set of black wrist cuffs. "I thought these would go better with your outfit than the blue ones." Gage buckled them in place.

"I love them! They're comfortable." Landry held his arms up, admiring his new cuffs.

"And a different collar." The strip of leather was much wider than the pale blue collar Landry often wore. "This one locks and there's a ring in front so I can attach a lead." Gage took off the St. Christopher Landry wore as his day collar then locked the new one in place. "Soon, I'm going to get you something more permanent. Something in metal that you can wear in the shower. It needs to be more secure than the St. Christopher."

"That would be amazing. I love wearing your necklace but this feels so good." Landry bounced on the bed. "This is turning me on."

"I can tell." Gage gave Landry's dick a pointed look.

"I can't help it!"

"But I can." When Landry stopped bouncing, Gage fitted a steel cock ring in place. "This should help you behave."

Landry pouted. "It's heavy.

"You can dress now. Unless a spanking would adjust your attitude?"

Landry attempted to look contrite. He didn't want to spend the evening with a sore ass. "No, Sir. Sorry."

"Two strokes with the cane when we get back later. I'll add one more for every infraction."

Landry didn't enjoy the cane as much as a paddle or tawse. He liked a thud and heat rather than sharp lines of fire the cane left on his skin. Gage's hand was even better. "Yes, Sir." Arguing would get him nowhere. Mules had nothing on Gage's level of stubborn.

"I showered at my place. I just have to change," Gage said.

Watching Gage pull on scuffed leather pants over a black jock made Landry deliriously happy. The tight black T-shirt seemed an excessive amount of clothing, but it did emphasize Gage's lean torso. *Perhaps he'll take it off later. It'll be hot at the club.* Landry smiled.

"What are you thinking about?" Gage asked, buckling his boots.

"You with no shirt on," Landry admitted. "It's tempting to suggest we stay home and get straight to the horizontal stuff."

"But then I won't get to see you in latex."

"True, and that would be a tragedy." After a liberal application of baby powder, Landry squirmed and wriggled his way into the shiny, short-sleeved body suit, which zipped to the neck and ended mid-thigh. A crotch zip would grant Gage access if he wanted it. Gage stared.

"You don't like it?" Landry did a twirl.

"It's…spectacular." Gage licked his lips. "I'm not going to be able to let you out of my sight, am I? That suit leaves very little to the imagination. Men are going to be lusting after you as soon as you walk through the door at Scorch." Gage circled behind Landry. He lowered the zipper, exposing Landry's ass. "I should plug this. I don't want anyone else thinking it's free for their use." He rubbed his thumb over Landry's hole. "Bend over."

Landry leaned over the bed, wondering which of Gage's extensive collection of plugs he'd brought along. "No one is going to get near my ass, Gage."

"Best to be safe."

"You just want an excuse."

Gage rummaged in his bag, apparently deciding between a few options. "Maybe. This one will do nicely. Not too hard but big enough you'll know it's there." Landry twisted his head to eye the egg-shaped toy. Gage doused it with lube then pressed it to Landry's hole. "Relax. Take it for me."

"Oh!" The widest part of the plug was quite a stretch but the sensation of being stuffed full sent shivers of pleasure through Landry's body. Gage zipped the suit closed then gave Landry's backside a pat, making him squeal. "Eggscellent. Now we can go."

Landry stood, hands on hips. "Did you just make the worst joke in the history of man?" Gage grinned. "For that, you should be the one getting the caning later. Unbelievable. My dad makes better jokes than that."

"Get your coat, Landry." Gage didn't stop smirking all the way to the car.

* * * *

Scorch lived up to its name. The dance floor was heaving and heat emanated from the packed press of semi-naked bodies. After dancing some and catching up with friends, most of them Landry's, Gage found a rare free table in a corner. Landry was content to kneel next to him for a while and indulge in some people watching. He wasn't uncomfortable—Gage had given him a pad to cushion his knees—but the plug and cock ring combination were driving him to distraction. He needed something to focus on other than the demands of his body. Gage chatted to two Doms he knew who had joined him at the table. Neither had a sub with him. Landry caught bits of their conversation but the music and crowds made it hard to hear—they seemed to be discussing a bespoke dungeon furniture maker from England that one of them had found online. Landry wondered if Gage was contemplating a kinky purchase and that gave his imagination something to work with.

Landry's attention was drawn by two of the club staff preparing a small stage area for a demonstration, positioning a padded St. Andrew's cross front and center. Curious, Landry waited to see what would happen. After a few minutes, the music volume lowered and a crowd of men gathered in front of the stage.

"Would you like to watch?" Gage asked. Landry's view of the stage was now blocked.

"If you would, Sir. It could be interesting."

Gage stood, holding out a hand. Landry took it and came gracefully to his feet. He followed Gage to a spot at the side of the stage where he had an unobstructed view. The hubbub of conversation died as a masked Dom led his sub, in a full head mask and blindfold, onto the stage. The sub was lithe, lightly muscled and walked like a dancer. Apart from the leather headgear, he wore a black silk thong and nothing else. Murmurs of appreciation rippled through the audience. The incognito Dom, clad in black leather pants, hooded jacket and boots, guided his sub to the cross where he chained him facing away from the crowd. The mask the Dom wore wouldn't have been out of place at a steampunk costume party. Fashioned from what looked like beaten metal, there were holes for his eyes, nostrils and mouth. The rest was embellished with all sorts of metal cogs, buttons and springs. It was an impressive, somewhat intimidating get-up.

"I think that mask the sub is wearing has an integral gag," Gage murmured. "I have one similar."

He can't see or speak. I doubt he can hear much either. That takes some trust. Landry looked for any sign that the sub was anxious but he seemed relaxed. There was no obvious tension in his frame. From his belt, the Dom uncoiled a multi-strand whip.

"Cat-o'-nine-tails," Gage said. "Not something to be used by an amateur."

"Will it break skin, Sir?" Landry asked, not sure he wanted to witness that.

"It could, but not necessarily. It can sting or thud depending on how it's wielded. It's much harsher than a flogger."

The Dom didn't speak but rotated his wrist until the whip flew in a figure eight, barely brushing the sub's skin. Even in the dim light, Landry could see color building until the sub's back and ass blushed pink. The Dom changed his strokes and the only sound was the whistle of multiple strands splitting the air, the thud of leather on skin and the increasing whimpers and cries of the bound man.

Landry flinched with every blow but Gage squeezed his shoulder, calming him. The whipping seemed to go on forever but finally the Dom lowered his arm. He untied the sub then turned him around to lean on the cross. He was hard but made no attempt to touch himself. The Dom flexed his fingers as if they were stiff from delivering the whipping then grasped the sub's rigid shaft in one fist. The sub came instantly, splattering the stage with glistening droplets, and there was a collective gasp from the audience.

"I love you." The Dom kissed his sub's bare shoulder then turned to survey the audience, his gaze resting briefly on Landry.

Landry turned to Gage. "Sir!"

"I know."

Landry swiveled back to the stage but both Dom and sub had gone.

"His accent when he said I love you…"

"British. The way he looked at you. Fuck." Gage took Landry back to their table. "Wait here. Don't move." He ran toward the door leading to the changing room and bathrooms.

Landry found it impossible to sit still, which didn't help when it came to the plug in his ass. He fidgeted, chewed his nails, ran his hands through his hair and scanned every part of the club he could see in the hope that Gage might reappear from a random direction. Three different Doms asked if he was okay. He was about to risk Gage's wrath and go looking for him when one of Scorch's bouncers, a man Landry knew by sight, came over and handed him a package.

"I didn't know it was your birthday. Many happy returns." The package was wrapped in birthday paper. "Your friends had to leave but asked me to pass this on."

"It's not my…" The bouncer was already striding back toward the exit. Landry put the gift on the table and stared at it like it might bite him. His relief when Gage reappeared manifested as a leap into his arms. Gage hugged him tight.

"I'm back. Everything's fine."

"You were gone so long! It was James Ellery, wasn't it? He was the Dom on stage. Tad was the sub."

"Yes. I saw them on the club's security feed leaving by a rear fire exit. They had a motorcycle parked in the alley." Gage sighed. "And he knew the camera was there. The bastard had the nerve to smile and wave."

"That display wasn't faked." Landry was certain about that. "Unlike his flirting with me."

"No. I'd say that was a pointed demonstration designed to tell me that they can do what they want, go where they want, and there's not a damn thing I can do about it."

"They left something for me too." Landry gestured to the gift.

Gage sat, putting Landry in his lap. "You should open it. Ellery has no need or desire to hurt you."

Landry picked up the shoe-box sized package. He tore off the paper then lifted the lid. Inside, snugly nestled in a bed of shredded paper was a lucky cat. There was a gift card tucked next to it. Landry took the card, putting the box back on the table.

"*An apology,*" he read. "*We hope this brings you better fortune than the last one.*"

Gage gave a low chuckle. "I have to admit, the man has style. I assume that's genuine?"

"I'd say so," Landry said, eyeing the cat. "Mr. Lao will be able to authenticate it, but it could be worth a lot of money. Did you know Ellery was a Dom?"

"Yes. One of the things I clarified that day he cooked breakfast at your apartment."

"And Tad is his sub. No wonder he was prepared to take such risks for him."

"That demonstration on stage confirmed the trust between them, wouldn't you say?"

Landry nodded and leaned into Gage's body. "A huge amount of trust. They must have been together some time. I think I'd like to go home now, Sir. You aren't going after them, are you?"

"Ellery wouldn't have come here without a foolproof escape plan. He's had a while to put this together. He took Tad from witness protection and avoided detection by several law enforcement agencies, all for a grand gesture. Pursuing him would be futile. Life's too short and I can think of far better ways to spend the rest of the night than chasing round the streets of Seattle hunting a man I'm never going to find."

"Me too. You know I trust you just as much as Tad trusts Ellery? I...I mean...I love you. I have for a while, I think...but I've never been in love before. Watching them on the stage...I wanted it to be us up there with a connection so deep that nothing else mattered." *I said it! Why did I say it? It's too soon.*

Gage tilted Landry's head so he could look into his eyes. "My sweet, adorable brat. I never thought I'd find someone to love. You proved me wrong."

Landry sniffled. "You're gonna make me cry. You really love me too?"

"I do. No tear stains on the leather." Gage slung Landry over his shoulder. "We're out of here."

"Don't forget my cat!"

Gage gave Landry's ass a sharp smack, agitating the plug. Landry yelped but grinned all the way to the street as applause and catcalls followed Gage's march across the club.

"Pretty sure they all know you're mine, now," Gage said.

"You think?" Landry had never felt safer or more loved.

* * * *

Landry sprawled on his bed, glad to be home. "I think I must be getting old. The club was fun but all I wanted was to be alone with you."

Gage stripped off his T-shirt. "It was noisy and crowded. We should start going on quiet nights when it's more about conversation and meeting friends than deafening music and dancing."

"Sounds good. I can't wait to get out of this suit. Peeling it off is almost as much fun as wearing it."

"And that pleasure is going to be mine." Barefoot but still wearing his leather pants, Gage got onto the bed, straddling Landry's thighs. He removed the cuffs first, answering Landry's quizzical glance with a low, "Trust me". He tugged at the zipper that ran from Landry's neck to his waist. "You'll have to polish the rubber—it has my fingerprints all over it." Landry squirmed as Gage explored his bare chest, tweaking his nipples into hard peaks. "Can you get out of it?"

It took some wriggling but Landry managed to peel the suit to his waist. "I'm a bit sticky."

"You'll be even stickier soon." Gage undid the crotch zipper and Landry's ringed cock sprang free. Gage plunged his mouth over Landry's straining shaft. He sucked a few times and Landry cursed the cock ring that prevented him from coming. Not that it would carry on being a barrier for long if Gage continued doing what he was doing. No cock ring in the world was going to prevent Landry from coming if Gage kept sucking.

"Turn over," Gage ordered. Landry, his head spinning, flopped onto his belly. Gage tugged the suit down until he was able to discard it. When he clambered off the bed, Landry whined.

"Don't go."

"I'm not." Gage returned with a cane in his hand. "You didn't think I'd forget this, did you?" Before Landry could respond, Gage brought the cane down in two sharp blows that crossed both of Landry's buttocks. Landry yelled as parallel lines of heat seared his skin and he kept yelling when Gage, having resumed his position on the bed, removed the plug, hauled Landry to his hands and knees then thrust his tongue into Landry's hole.

"Fuck!" Landry's mind couldn't process the combination of pleasure and pain. He reached for his cock, desperate to come.

"Don't you dare!" Gage carried on rimming and probing while Landry squirmed and clawed at the sheets. He lost track of how long Gage tormented him but when he stopped, Landry sobbed. He bounced a little as Gage moved off the bed and Landry craned his neck to watch Gage struggling free of his pants and jock.

"Thank you, Lord." Landry struggled to remain in position, limbs trembling. "I'll never be bad again."

Gage spanked him right where the cane had left its marks and while Landry was breathing through the renewed pain, Gage thrust into him. Slick from the plug, Landry squeezed his inner muscles, clenching around Gage's cock.

"Tight." Gage grunted, pumping his hips. He withdrew then flipped Landry onto his back. He lifted one of Landry's legs onto his shoulder then twisted him to the side. The new position allowed him even deeper penetration and Landry whimpered.

"Please...please, Sir!"

Gage fumbled with the cock ring, cursing. "Damn lube made my hands slippery." He managed to get it free and Landry took deep gulping breaths. There was no way he could hold back. He came with a yell, shocked at the ferocity of his orgasm. His vision blurred around the edges and his entire body shook. Gage came too, growling through his release even while gripping Landry's cock, squeezing every last drop of fluid from Landry's sated body. For a while they lay there, the only sound their heavy breathing.

Gage withdrew but Landry was only empty for as long as it took Gage to reinsert the plug. "Gonna keep my seed inside you all night. Don't move."

Landry wasn't sure he could even if he wanted to. He had ended up on his belly, head turned so he could breathe. He eyed Gage, who returned clutching some short lengths of rope.

"What are you...?"

"You'll see. This is why I took the cuffs off." Gage bound Landry's legs together at the knees and ankles. He used the last piece of rope to tie his wrists, attaching the free end to the headboard. "There. No chance you'll get rid of that plug now." He massaged Landry's ass, pressing the cane marks. Landry was half-hard again already, the restrictive bondage, Gage's scent on his skin, the hint of pain all combining to put him in a dream-like state of ecstasy.

"I love you, Landry Carran." Gage lay down, pulling the covers over them. "I love my scent on your skin, my marks on your body."

"I love you too," Landry murmured, catching sight of the line of lucky cats on the shelf next to the bed, their paws raised like they were offering high-fives.

They were smiling.

Want to see more from this author? Here's a taster for you to enjoy!

The Retreat: Serving Him
L.M. Somerton

Excerpt

"Who'd have thought there would be so many applicants for a role where the job description includes nudity and a willingness to get your arse whipped?" Carey Hoffman leafed through the pile of paperwork in front of him. "This is a lot harder than recruiting for club servers."

"Relax, Sir. It's important we find the right people. The more applicants we get, the better chance we have of finding someone perfect." Alistair Easton, Carey's submissive, kneaded his Master's shoulders. "Our first paying client deserves the best."

"That's so good." The tension melted from Carey's shoulders as Alistair loosened knotted muscles. "Maybe we should go upstairs for an hour so that you can relieve other parts of my anatomy."

Alistair giggled. "Not a good idea if you want to invite people in for interviews this week. We have work to do."

Scowling, Carey turned to his friend and bar manager Harry Croft. "What's a Dom to do, Harry, when his sub takes charge?"

"Generally," Harry replied, "I find it's best to do what I'm told." He ruffled his sub's hair. Kai Smithson was seated on the floor between Harry's legs. "You can always spank him later, but for now, Alistair is right. We have to get through all these applications this evening. We only have one post left to fill, don't we?"

Alistair knelt at Carey's side, hands folded in his lap, his serenity in complete contrast to the noise and activity going on all around them. The Underground was always busy, but Friday nights tended to be hectic. Carey had sequestered a quiet corner for their discussion. A low table held paperwork and drinks, and cushions softened the floor for Alistair's knees and Kai's backside. Carey still found it hard to concentrate. He blamed Alistair for looking so tempting in leather trousers and a sheer silk shirt. He imagined removing the shirt, exposing Alistair's smooth skin inch by inch, then watching his lover wriggle out of the trousers...

"Carey?" Harry brought him out of his daydream.

"Sorry, I got a bit distracted. Where were we?"

"The last vacancy — if you can keep your mind on recruitment and off whatever it is you're planning to do to Alistair?" He shared a conspiratorial grin.

"Oh, yes. Right. Well, I'm thankful Mr. Wilder's requirements are not too onerous. Tor Halvorsen will act as executive chef. He cooked for Joe and Heath when they had their taster weekend with Olly and Aiden and their reviews of his cooking were first rate. Olly said, and I'm quoting here, that Tor's double chocolate brownies were better than an orgasm after two days in chastity."

Alistair and Kai both burst out laughing.

Harry rolled his eyes. "Olly would be proud. He can create chaos even when he's hundreds of miles away. That's two extra strokes for you tonight, young man." He gave Kai's hair a gentle tug. Kai sucked on his lower lip but his eyes sparkled and he rubbed his cheek against Harry's thigh.

"Tor has recruited two kitchen assistants, both, I might add, stolen from here at The Underground," Carey said. "As Mr. Wilder is traveling alone, Tor says that will be more than adequate to cover his stay and allow for days off for each of them. Tor intends to work through and take some time off in between clients. He'll also take on training Benjy and Frank. Going forward, I think we should consider rotating the junior kitchen staff through The Retreat. Then they'll all get experience of different kinds of catering."

"That's a great idea. At least they won't be shocked by anything they see at The Retreat." Harry grinned. "Right. Goran has sorted all the drink supplies, so Mr. Wilder won't starve or go thirsty." Goran was Harry's very capable deputy bar manager. "He can always take a quick trip down there if Tor needs him for anything. It's always possible that the client will want to throw a party while he's staying. Goran's already offered to run the bar for events like that."

Carey nodded. "Excellent. Then we have Luke Redding as general manager. He's ex-forces, like Tor."

"The Retreat is going to be run like a military campaign," Harry said. "Tell me about Luke. I know he's a member here but not much else."

"He's a well-respected Dom. Kept up his membership even when he was overseas on active duty."

"Well, you do give service personnel an excellent discount."

"I do, and they deserve it. Whereas Tor was in the army, Luke is ex-Navy. Served fifteen years then took an honorable discharge to care for his father who died last year. Mother passed when he was a child so his dad brought him up. He told me at the interview that he gave himself to his career, then to his father, now it's his time. He was very open. He doesn't have to work for the money but needs a purpose. He's a very experienced manager and won't take shit from anyone. He'll be perfect for mentoring the young men that will be working at The Retreat, as well as the contractors. Management of the house and garden staff as well as all the arrangements related to housekeeping and maintenance will sit with him, and if our guests want any training in a particular technique, Luke can either handle it himself or bring someone in from the club if he doesn't feel qualified. He knows the area well too — he was based at Portsmouth for many years and the New Forest was a favorite daytrip destination."

"I hope I'll get to meet him one day," Harry said. "I'm surprised I've never come across him here."

"I'm sure you will. I intend to have post-stay debriefings with The Retreat's management team here at the club."

"Good idea. So, when you Skyped with Mr. Wilder…"

"Lorcan. He prefers to be called Lorcan."

"When you Skyped with Lorcan, did he have any special requirements for other staff?"

"I think he's going to be a low maintenance client — he was reserved, but friendly. The stay is a personal reward for selling his business. From what I could make out, he's done little else but work for many years. He's had some training as a Dominant and has excellent references from a couple of clubs I know in the U.S. He wants to see whether immersion in the lifestyle is what he wants because, as he said, he thinks it is but he's never had time to prove it to himself."

"Sounds like he has his head in the right place."

Nodding, Carey flicked through a few applications. "I've done a full background check. There was an incident in his late teens, which I won't go into here because it shouldn't cause any issues. It marks him as a survivor. He plays hard when he has the time but that isn't often. He admits to a preference for blonds. Smaller than him and not too muscled."

"How tall is he?" Harry asked.

"Six feet one."

"That rules out three of these—all within an inch of that height. There are also several brunets and one redhead in here so I'll put them aside. That still leaves six possibles."

"Whoever we choose has to be prepared to be very flexible." At Harry's feet, Kai giggled. "Not that kind of flexible, brat," Carey chided. "Lorcan wants one man to be his personal assistant, valet and submissive. He doesn't want a lot of people around the place because his break is about getting some breathing space, so this man will be at his beck and call twenty-four seven. Experience isn't needed. I think Lorcan wants someone he can mold to his requirements, so we're looking for a relative innocent—but one who knows what he's getting into."

"And who understands the difference between furniture wax and candle wax." Harry rolled his eyes. "Talk about mission impossible."

"The housework will be light, just Lorcan's bedroom and bathroom. The contracted cleaning service will handle the rest. We'll need someone bright enough to be an effective assistant..."

"And who doesn't mind taking notes naked, with a plug up his arse." Harry laughed. "Sorry, I'm being facetious."

"You may not be that far off the mark. Nudity and minimal dress are nonnegotiable."

"Well, that helps us narrow the field a bit more. Two of these applicants are house subs here. I know them both and I don't think either of them could be called sweet and innocent—they're a pair of brats. Of the remaining four, two have university degrees and one went to work straight from school but got very good grades at A level. The last one seems to have drifted from job to job but does have waiting experience."

"Drop him for now and ask the other three to come in. When we have time, I want to see all the applicants we've rejected for this job in case they'd like us to hold their details for future opportunities. It would be nice to be able to offer clients a portfolio of staff to choose from rather than having to go through this process all the time. That way we can also broach the subject when we recruit staff for The Underground. Whoever we choose this time will be permanently employed, but The Retreat is fully booked for months. We'll need to alternate between clients so that the houseboys can take some time off and that means we need to line up someone else for the next booking after Mr. Wilder. We can cover unexpected illness or, God forbid, walk-outs, with staff from the club in the meantime." Carey caught Alistair's eye. "What do you think, love?"

"The catalogue is a brilliant idea. I'd be happy to take pictures for it, but maybe you should ask some of the members what they think, too? You have an instant audience for research here."

"You're right, of course." Carey surveyed his club. The Underground was his pride and joy and he fully intended to make The Retreat just as perfect. "I'll leave the interview arrangements to you, Harry. Time for me to make sure my members are happy. I think the boss giving his sub a public spanking might go down well tonight, don't you?"

"You know it will."

At Carey's side, Alistair shivered. Carey stroked his hair. "Would you like that, sweetheart?"

"If it makes you happy, Sir." Alistair kept his eyes downcast but Carey could see he was smiling.

"Oh, it will, you can be sure of that and if you're very, very good you might even get to come. Emphasis on the *might*." Carey raised his glass. "A toast. Here's to finding someone for Lorcan Wilder who lives up to our exacting standards."

Harry pulled Kai onto his lap. He clinked his glass against Carey's. "Bottoms up!" He avoided spilling his drink by the narrowest margin as Kai shook with laughter.

"They soon will be." Carey chuckled while Alistair tried, unsuccessfully, to conceal a groan.

PUBLISHING

Sign up for our newsletter and find out about all our romance book releases, eBook sales and promotions, sneak peeks and FREE romance books!

About the Author

Lucinda lives in a small village in the English countryside, surrounded by rolling hills, cows and sheep. She started writing to fill time between jobs and is now firmly and unashamedly addicted.

She loves the English weather, especially the rain, and adores a thunderstorm. She loves good food, warm company and a crackling fire. She's fascinated by the psychology of relationships, especially between men, and her stories contain some subtle (and some not so subtle) leanings towards BDSM.

Lucinda loves to hear from readers. You can find her contact information, website details and author profile page at https://www.pride-publishing.com

www.ingramcontent.com/pod-product-compliance
Lightning Source LLC
Chambersburg PA
CBHW050730180626
46814CB00002B/683